The Soul Trek

This book is a work of fiction. The characters, incidents, and dialogues are products of the author's imagination and are not to be construed as real. Any resemblance to actual events or persons, living or dead, is entirely coincidental.

Edited by Spica Aldebaran
All rights reserved.

First published in 2010

www.thesoultrek.com

Copyright © 2010 Djana Fahryeva
All rights reserved.

ISBN: 1-4505-4475-4
ISBN-13: 9781450544757

The Soul Trek

A Story of Love, Faith and Destiny

Djana Fahryeva

www.thesoultrek.com

2010

Dedication

For my Angels.

Contents

Volume I
A Story of Love

Deep within time. Blue:printed in reality
Our minds intwine in the race for The Ultimate.

The multiversity of existence slows down<
A gateway opens>
Tibetan Buddhism brings us together in linear time.

You and I come from different countries, different religious back-
grounds and separate continents.
You and I recognize each other and read other's minds. You and I are
One.
We travel to ancient places of worship, exploring our heritage.

Looking into each other's eyes - a chemical reaction taking us beyond
dimensions

to our Single Soul's Mission <>

...I always feared I could die without knowing what it is like to love someone. And now I am crossing over. Gigantic feather wings take me in their loving embrace. The land is barren....the soil is cracked...the water has dried out. An essence stands next to me.

Why am I still <u>here</u>.

You don't know me yet, but you have felt me your entire life, as I have felt you. We have been created as One, but separated to live our lives apart and experience third-dimension until we are ready to re-unite. I see you in my dreams. I wake up feeling the longing, yearning for our love.

- Where are you? – asked my mother. I had been sobbing as we sat in a kids playground on a sunny May day in Moscow.
- It is time. He is searching for me.
- What are you talking about?
- My other half.
- Who is it?
- Me.

May I become at all times, both now and forever
A protector for those without protection
A guide for those who have lost their way
A ship for those with oceans to cross
A bridge for those with rivers to cross
A sanctuary for those in danger
A lamp for those without light
A place for refuge for those who lack shelter
and a servant to all in need.

- His Holiness the Dalai Lama the XIV

I. Exile.

The flight attendant hands me a lunch of fish curry. It makes me sick and brings me pain. My entire life I've felt incomplete. A void within me that needed to be filled with another part of me. But we couldn't *be*. I travel the world looking for the slightest reminder of what being with you felt like. I *miss* you. My heart and my love belong to you, always have, and love is all we are here for and being <u>here</u> makes no sense.

The Monastery was established in 1979 by Lama Thubten Yeshe and Lama Zopa Rinpoche. Monks and nuns from all over Nepal, Tibet, Bhutan and India live and study here. It is a retreat center for international students to study, meditate and attend discussions groups. It is part of the Foundation for the Preservation of the Mahayana Tradition, an international network of one hundred forty five centers dedicated to the study and practice of Buddhism.

The Mahayana tradition comes from the word "maha" - which means greater and "yana" which means vehicle. This tradition of Buddhism is prevalent through Tibet, Mongolia, China, Korea and Japan, emphasizing the attainment of complete liberation of all sentient beings from obscurations and sufferings. Another tradition is Hinayana - which means Lesser Vehicle and is practiced in Burma, Thailand, Laos and less in Cambodia and Vietnam - emphasizing the four truths and related teachings through which an individual seeks his own salvation, rather than the elimination of other's sufferings. Thus its goal is more self-centered and lacks a full understanding of emptiness.

There is another, higher vehicle - the Vajrayana - the Diamond Vehicle which emphasizes the fruitional tantra teachings and meditative techniques concerning the unbroken mental continuum from ignorance to enlightenment. Tantra is a body of beliefs that the Universe we experience is a manifestation of the divine energy, which seeks to channel that energy within the human microcosm.

Our course is 7 days during which we must abide by the rules of the monastery. Our food will be served three times a day and each student must volunteer to help in washing dishes. Our teacher is Ani Agata - a Swedish nun who found the monastery twenty years ago when she went backpacking. She took refuge in the Buddha, the Dharma and the Sangha and after years of study and dedicated practice, she became ordained. All the nuns and monks have shaven heads and wear crimson red robes. They have no source of income, and they are not allowed to marry.

We will be meditating twice every day - in the morning before breakfast, followed by teachings , lunch, and a discussion group. Then dinner; and another meditation in the evening before bedtime.

Ani Agata tells us the story of the Buddha - who was born in the North-East of India that is now the small village of Lumbini in Nepal - eight hours East of Kathmandu. His mother Maya had given birth to him under a tree during a voyage. His father King Suddhodhana of the Sakya clan had surrounded him with pleasures and luxuries of royal life in the palace; and an astrologer had predicted he would become a powerful king one day. His birth name was Siddhartha. He had lived in the palace and got married and had a child by twenty-nine years of age. One day he saw an old man crippled by disease and disorder. He questioned, what was wrong with him? The old man told him he was suffering. The Prince wondered, what is suffering? He ventured outside the palace walls to see the lives of ordinary people, *full* of suffering: hunger, poverty, disease. He left the palace and his family, and a kingdom and throne he would take over and went to live as a sage and itinerant monk - Gautama. In strict asceticism, he had starved himself until he was skin and bones. And then he realized this is not the way to achieve enlightenment. So he began to eat again and built his strength. He meditated with other sages and attained enlightenment on the forty-ninth day under the Boddhi Tree. Hence his name - Sakyamuni Buddha - the Enlightened Sage of the Sakya clan. He then developed the Middle Way - the Four Noble Truths. That is, in all life there is suffering. Suffering is caused by desire and attachment. To end suffering one must transcend desire and attachment. In order to do so one must follow the Eightfold Path. Which consists of the Right View, the Right Resolve, the Right Speech, the Right Action, the Right Livelihood, the Right Effort, the Right Mindfulness and the Right Concentration.

I sit outside the gompa and talk to an American guy from St. Louis. He is surprised to learn that I know where St. Louis is. He is not taking part in the course, he is re-treating: relaxing at the monastery and reading. I tell him about my friend who talked to Angels.

I return to my dorm to meet two of my roommates - Anka from Poland and Tina from Salt Lake City. Anka had just come from India and graphically narrates about the toilet system. Tina had just come down from Pokhara where she and her boyfriend did the Annapurna trek. As she goes on and on about how amazing it had been to sleep in tents and wake up to see the sun rising over one of the most beautiful trails in the world - I feel more and more stupid to have come here to sit and meditate and miss out on the adventure.

I will change residences so I can be by myself in order to focus and think properly. Let's see if I can do it. Easy. It is private but full of ants! Oh well. I notice a spark. I see a familiarity. I walked in, "mind if I join you?". I am suddenly hit with a haze of reminiscence. Jump in, excited, smiling, showing his pearly white teeth, a sign of good genetic heritage. "Is that one of those chocolates"?! He spurted out. "Yeah, with cookies inside" I reply. "Yeah I know I love 'em!"

Inside the Gompa I carefully examine the thangkas — uniquely Tibetan cloth-painted scrolls invested with the spirit of a deity to whom they are consecrated. They are also ritual artifacts. They are normally offered with a *khata* – a Tibetan white sacred scarf. It symbolizes clarity of mind. Offerings include oil lamps and bowls of water, which are changed everyday by a Gompa keeper, while we have our lunch. There are 5 rules at the monastery: no killing, no lying, no stealing, no intoxicants and no sexual activity. One must also take off their shoes before entering the meditation hall.

OM AH HUM - OM AH HUM - OM AH HUM

The Chenrezig Gompa is decorated with deity statues. They are encrusted with gold – also symbolic for clarity of mind. The statues' hand positioning is very significant – the mudras – each hand gesture is symbolic of either protection, a blessing, a greeting, teaching or refuge. If you do them yourself – they create certain energetic twists in the body, stimulate blood flow to the needed organs, and activate energy flows. A big statue of the Buddha with the Dharmachakra mudra - the Wheel of Law hand gesture is looking back at me. The first two fingers of each hand are closed together across from each other, and the rest of the fingers are widely spread out. The three extended fingers of the left hand symbolize the Three Jewels of Buddhism - the Buddha, the Dharma, and the Sangha. In this mudra, the hands are held in front of the heart, symbolizing that these teachings are straight from the Buddha's heart.

I walk around the amazing setting within the Kathmandu Valley. On clear days one can see the Boudhanath. There are many prayer wheels which you can spin just walking by. They contain sacred mantras - syllables or prayers, the power of which is activated by the spinning motion of the wheel. Every spin of every wheel is a mantra once read, and sent out to heaven. A man-tra literally means mind-protection. It is protecting the mind from insignificant outside influences by recitation of incantations associated with various meditational deities, thereby speaking Buddha-speech. *Protecting the self from the mind, but also protecting the mind from the self.* **For the benefit of all sentient beings....**

OM MANI PADME HUM

The Main Gompa is typical Tibetan Buddhist architecture of white-washed walls and crimson roofs decorated with a huge golden Wheel of Law with two deer flanking it. It is the symbol of Mahayana Buddhism. The deer remind me of the Capitoline wolf who fed Romulus and Remus: two brothers in a competition for superiority. A fight for approval by the powers that be, like Kayin and Hevel: a shepherd and a farmer.

As I walk through the alleys behind the canteen I see lamas carrying prayer beads in their hands - for relaxation of mind. The rosaries - prayer beads - consist of 108 beads, representing the 108 human passions that Avalokiteshvara is believed to have assumed when telling the beads.

...I explore the *debri* - mural paintings on the walls of the prayer hall. Small statues of the female deity of Tara make it look surreal... as the Taras float atop little clouds... The circle in the prayer hall reminds me of the energy wheels in our bodies. It is like a model of Universe = a powerful meditational and healing tool. Art speaks more than words, and Tibetan works of art serve primarily as icons, intermediaries between man and divinity, a function underscored by the indigenous term *tongdrol* - liberation by seeing the deity. In conjunction with ritual, a painting houses a deity consecrated for purposes of worship, offering, meditative visualization and spiritual communication.

The second day of the course begins with a meditation at 6.30 in the morning. Apparently we are lucky, as many retreats start at 4 in the morning. We have breakfast and start class at 9.

Contemplating on your life
Death and rebirth are One aspect
Be aware of impermanence

Remember...

Think of that thing and ask yourself out of what I did it: anger, attachment or ignorance

Perhaps remorse

Guilt has no other purpose but to make you feel

If you want to know your past, look into your body

If you want to know the future, look at your present mind

I bought a pack of cigarettes – a bad excuse and response to stressing over humidity. I need to shower all the time – and once I'm clean, I'm sweaty again. I was always the clean one, the obsessive-compulsive type of clean one.

I walk into the library building and up the stairs. From here, I see the gate of the monastery's site and the road leading to the main building which is decorated with a drawing of a lotus and an umbrella. There is also a wheel – the Wheel of Dharma. They are three of the 8 auspicious symbols of Tibetan Buddhism. A monk explains to me that what I see as a joining of the squares actually forms an Endless Knot - the intertwining of lines, meant to remind us how all phenomena are conjoined as a closed cycle of cause and effect - the composition is a pattern that is closed on in itself with no gaps, leading to a representational form of great simplicity and fully balanced harmony.

Because all phenomena are interrelated, the placing of the endless knot is meant to establish an auspicious connection between the giver and the recipient. At the same time, the recipient is goaded to righteous karma, being reminded that future positive effects have their roots in the causes of the present. The knot represents a connection, a link with our fates, binding us to our karmic destiny.

A monk in the monastery shop tells me that the 8 auspicious symbols are "promising success and good fortune" – and are given for New Years or a birthday. I buy a set. One of the symbols is the two fishes that collide whereas my sun sign of Pisces is two fishes swimming in opposite directions but both pulled by one string. In Buddhism, the golden fishes symbolize happiness, as they have complete freedom in water; fertility and abundance as they multiply rapidly.

I go back to the library and start searching. Searching for the right book and the right connection on a bookshelf is like searching for your answer within the grid. The course of my destiny. I find a book with ancient sutras. It describes the lotus, the parasol, the treasure vase, the victory banner and the conch shell.

At the evening meditation class, the smell of juniper incense burning as we sit down and hold our palms together in the dhyani position – the gesture of a person in meditation and the gesture of samadhi. It closes the energy circuit in the body – the energy stays within the system.

Ani Agata guides us through a visualization meditation on the Avalokiteshvara thangka - one of the eight major boddhi-sattvas - Enlightened Beings - and the patron deity of Tibet, symbolizing the Buddha's compassion and holding a lotus untainted by flaws. He has 11 faces and 1,000 arms. As we meditate on the light emanating from him and visualize a lotus opening underneath our seats...

Buddhists believe that just as the lotus flower rises from the depths of muddy ponds and lakes to blossom immaculately above the water's surface, the human heart or mind can develop the virtues of the Buddha and transcend desires and attachments, to reveal its successful Buddha nature. The unopened lotus = the lotus bud = is symbolic of the potential of all beings to attain buddhahood or enlightenment...

...in esoteric Buddhism the heart is often compared with an unopened lotus...when the virtues of the Buddha develop within the heart, the heart blossoms like a lotus.

..a strong pressure on my forehead. It is very powerful. The energy in the monastery is very high.

After the class I get up and walk to one of the prayer halls where only monks are allowed. I believe this is the building where the relics of one of the Lama's are kept. A tooth. And a string of hair. I sit outside and listen to the prayers.

I cry as the prayers linger the sensitive strings in my soul.
It starts to rain.

A monk takes pity on me and gives me his raincoat and I run to my room.

Day 3.

Ani Agata explains the significance of the bowl as offering in Buddhism. It goes back to the legend when the Buddha was meditating under a tree, a woman saw him and offered him a bowl of rice. He had divided it in 49 heaps, one for each day of the path to enlightenment. Because a monk cannot possess anything, he had put the bowl in the river and it floated away. Thus the simple food bowl is often regarded to as the Buddha and his teachings.

The Buddhist Mandala is the topic of our day. It is literally a circle or arc, representing the entire sacred universe, and symbolic expression of Buddhist cosmology. They serve as teaching devices for initiated practitioners. The dimension of symbolism of the mandala is incorporated in the design and placement of buildings of Tibetan Buddhist temples. It has been noted that the mandala embraces the totality of awareness, from an entire cosmic vision to a dwelling and the human body as well.

The best known mandala is the Kalachakra mandala - the Wheel of Time. A sand mandala, for which colored sand grains are painstakingly placed. The sand drawing represents a 3D palace. Every single detail thereof has a symbolic meaning. A mandala is a symbolic representation of many aspects of a specific tantra. In the Kalachakra tantra, all elements of the mandala refer to the universe, the body and mind and the practice - initiation, generation and completion stages.

Every detail of the mandala, from each deity to every adornments of the building, refers to time and the universe, physical and mental aspects of Kalachakra and ourselves, and also to aspects of the practice.

The word mandala can be translated as "essence-containing" and it is destructed after it is completed....to symbolize the impermanence of all things.

There is no talking until after lunch. I take a few photos around.
I also take a lot of notes in my newly bought brown notebook off the monastery's bookshop. It is made of "lokta" paper and the cover is decorated with four triangles.

If I want to be out of samsara, I should liberate myself. I created the cause for this to happen.

If I get angry at a person, I only create suffering for myself. I can increase my anger or increase my compassion. Anger hurts. Anger is destroying the world. I don't want to become an angry person. I want to become a patient, compassionate person. So practice Dharma.

Only one person can teach me non-violence and patience - the enemy. We need the enemy to teach us tolerance and patience.

10

You are so kind you have become my teacher. Thank you for coming my away.

If someone is standing in your way, they are already hurting. So they are an object of compassion.

If you see - you do not have an object of anger, you have an object of compassion.

...your mind is still holding on to something...

a grudge remaining....so then you say, okay, I am the object of compassion. My grudge doesn't bother other people, it only poisons myself. It is the most foolish thing in the world. If you want to practice compassion, just let it go. release it.

Develop genuine compassion. If I can overcome this I can overcome any conflict.

The greatest protector is tolerance and compassion. When a person harms you he gains power over you. If you hate him or are angry at him, he gains power of you twice. To overcome that we develop compassion. He is hurt and unhappy.

The mind moves through lifetimes and carriers the memory. I ask out of the audience, isn't it the soul? No, the mind moves through lifetimes, not the soul. Buddhism does not recognize the term "soul".

When Tenzin Gyatso - the present Dalai Lama the XIV had been asked whether he is angry with the Chinese for having taken over his land, he said that he is very sorry for them, and that they will suffer the karma they have inflicted on themselves for their actions.

For him it is more important to have the ability to continue spreading universal compassion and non-violence. India is so generously offering land for them to be able to preserve the tradition.

I take my *thali* - a metal plate divided into compartments. I have lunch with one of my ex-roommates. I feel no connection. Guys had been making eye contact with me but all I talked to them about was how much the humidity bothers me. It is the sweating I hardly deal with.

Our lunch consists of daal baht - lentils, rice and mixed vegetables, sometimes with tofu, and always with plenty of spices and herbs. It hurts my stomach as I am not used to this food.

The discussion class is something else as the students talk about the commonality of all religions. But I feel a genuine connection between the Buddhist teachings and the film Matrix. The connection between mind, soul and the electromagnetic grid: the information field/endless knot/Akashic record.

Our evening meditation and visualization practice on the Amitabha thangka - "The One of Infinite Light" - one of the five peaceful meditational buddhas forming the buddha-body of perfect resources. He is red in color symbolizing the purity of perception and the discerning aspect of buddha-mind. He holds a lotus to symbolize the purification of attachment and the altruistic intention.

As I walk back to my room, I pay close attention to the prayer flags fluttering in the wind. They are arranged in blue, white, red, green and yellow, symbolizing the five elements: space, water, fire, air and earth. In each corner of the flag there is a protective animal: garuda (a large mythical bird), dragon, tiger and lion. The animals represent the qualities and attitudes necessarily developed on the spiritual path to enlightenment. Such as, awareness, vast vision, confidence, joy, humility and power. Each of the five colors of the prayer flags represents an element and an aspect of the enlightened mind.

Day 4.

The morning meditation follows a tea, a breakfast, and one of the help kicking a dog resting outside the canteen hard in the gut. It squeaks in pain!! I burst in tears and run away.

...I am on time for the class on ethics, poverty, hunger, helping the needy, applying the Buddha's teachings in the lives of beggars. We must help those who need help. I ask out of the audience how is it that we can intrude into their destiny? Don't they have karma to work out?

-       Do you believe you should not help them?
-       That's...not what I asked...I asked whether it is okay to intrude into their destiny.

Ani Agata narrates on one of the murals on the Main Gompa - that of the running mind. It is a coil-like path with different animals on a green background. The symbolism of this painting depicts the taming of the mind through meditation. The rabbit or hare is a symbol of the subtle aspects of the mental factor of sinking or subtle torpor. The practitioner is running after a black elephant. The hook that the practitioner carries is awareness. The rope is mindfulness. The elephant is the meditator's mind. The black color in the elephant is sinking or sleepiness. Attention or mindfulness is scattered by the pictured sense objects: taste - food, touch - cloth, sound - musical instruments, smell - perfume, vision - mirror. As the elephant's color becomes lighter, the white denotes progress in grasping the object of meditation and prolonged fixing of the mind on the object. The monkey is the scattering of the mind - which is the one the elephant is running after. The practitioner gets a grip on the elephant - hence taming of the mind - due to the fire depicted above the monkey and elephant and represents the energy of concentration. Finally, the practitioner tames the elephant - the mind - and sits atop him - with a sword as representation of the realization of emptiness....

...after the class I make a detour to the shop to buy a chocolate bar with little bits of biscuit. The discussion group the day before made me feel uncomfortable as one of the girls who looks like a gypsy in her Indian clothes with little mirrors to reflect the energy which is sent to her BACK to the person who sent it, was giving me a bad vibe. I believe the right thing to do was to detach., move away Move on to another discussion class and see what they are talking about.

- Do you guys mind if I join you?
- No, not at all! Jump in!

Cute guy with blue eyes in a bandana.

- Is this one of those chocolates with cookies?
- Uh, yes. It's from the shop. I love it.
- Yeah me too!!

There is something so incredibly familiar about the deep blue eyes, the blue bandana, the wide shoulders and beautiful arms. The tone of his voice and the way he smiles when he gets excited. Everything is so incredibly familiar. Where have I see him? Someone else there too. A girl. Short. Thin. Black hair.

- We have to warn you, we're very boring. We don't talk.
- Oh don't worry I can do the talking.

Who is this guy? Where is he from? I can't understand. English is his first language. But what country? Jesus. Where did he come from.

Time is streaming

<<<<<<

it is moving so fast

>>>>>>>

are we in the past? In the future? Is this a glimpse into the future?

- What are you doing here? - asks Ani Agata, as she is checking that everyone is actually showing up for discussion groups, not taking naps.
- I'd like to check out what everyone else is talking about, I hope that's okay.

She says it is ok and with my peripheral vision I notice how the guy who is giving me all these new vibes ducks his head down as his body speaks of affection.

The discussion is about helping others, having compassion and love for other human beings.

- You should never help someone until they ask you for help, says Anson — an older guy, here on a retreat.
- Yes, I agree. This is what my teacher taught me first thing — never help anyone until they ask you to. You can't keep on bumming into people's lives saying, "I'm gonna save you".
- Why not? - asks the cute guy with blue eyes.
- Because it drains the life out of you. Helping someone who can't be helped.
- What do you mean exactly? — asks a blonde English guy, - Like, can you give an example?
- It comes from personal experience.
- Tell us!
- Its kinda personal. I can't tell..

...when I over-dozed on Zoloft.

- I don't geddit. So if you see someone being raped, do you save them?
- Of course!
- But how is that not the same? — asks a girl.
- It's not the same. It is just that you get hit back for intruding into a destiny...
- Yeah — I know I agree with that, - says Anson. — I once stepped into a fight for a girl who was being treated badly by her boyfriend. And another day I was coming out of my house and his friends surrounded me and beat me up. That's when I knew that was my lesson.
- I think it is burnt off now though.
- Yeah.
- But I disagree that there is no soul! We are all souls...and I came from a soul source!!
- Well...I think you have a belief of your own...and you get defensive because you think the Buddhist philosophy

threatens your belief. I would advise you to just experience this as a new education.

He's good.

I let my hair loose.

The blue eye boy looks at me. I look at him.

Our souls speak of mutual interest and affection through our eyes.

Subtle. Natural. Intimate.

-    Things you don't like in other people are the things going on inside of you.
-    How is that?
-    Think about it. Like me, for example, I don't like skinny girls because I am not skinny. I don't like when people slouch because I slouch.
-    Really...that's how I always sit! - he jumps up in his seat.
-    Well this was fun, thanks for coming around, you made this interesting, - says Anson.
-    Thank you too. I enjoyed your group.

I want to keep the little sheet of paper with the questions on the agenda. The cute guy has it.

-    Can I have the paper with the questions?
-    Yeah…
-    Unless you want it.
-    No, no.
-    I just want to keep it for memory.

...we start to walk on to the meditation hall for the class.

-    Where are you from?
-    Moscow.
-    Wow, I was wondering where you were from. I was like, this girl just has a little bit of accent…Wow, I've been to Saint-Petersburg.
-    Where are you from?
-    America…
-    Wooo where's that.

There's something familiar in the way he said America. Why not the United States? So familiar in his accent and voice tone. His walk, his ways, everything, such a déjà vu. Deja sensi.

- What is your name?
- Djana.
- How do you spell that..?
- I just use J-a-n-a for the States usually.

...suddenly information starts coming. A spark of light streaming through the Earth's grid. Speak

- Did you live in one state, and then move to another?
- Yeah. California.
- Are you from California?
- No...I moved to California for six months, then returned home.
- Let me guess...Don't tell me...You are from...North...or North-West state?
- No...
- Erhm...
- The East Coast. New Jersey.
- Like thats what I said! It is North-East!
- Whatever you want to think!

...as we enter the Gompa, both in a whirlwind of recognition and excitement, he stands leaning on a pillar.

- So where are you from?
- New Jersey.

I've only seen five movies by Kevin Smith. They are all set in New Jersey.

- Why do they say negative mean things about New Jersey in movies and stuff?
- Oh it is 'cus there's the New Jersey turnpike, which is like the very ugly highway, with industrial enterprises around it. The place I'm from, the town is a great place, one hour from New York City and one hour from the beach.

I'm smiling...the beach..

- Do you like the beach?
- I love the beach. I want to get married on the beach.
- I know, I do.
- ...wearing this! - as he points at his rags of a green t-shirt torn and sweaty.
- Ooumph...maybe. How about...a swimsuit?

...he is in his world. But where *is* his world.

- What is your star sign?
- Scorpio.
- When is your birthday?
- November 21.

Serpentarius. The Snake-Carrier. The Sun. His father.
He must be a couple of years older than me. Maybe 24.

- What year?
- '78.

Saturn's return.

- So what made you take this journey? You're not 20...

Puzzled/pissed off grin...I'm trying to understand. How is it that he is so familiar.

- What is your name?
- James.
- It's a nice name.
- I didn't like it.
- What are you wearing?
- This? – points at his bandana.
- No.
- This? – points at his t-shirt.

...he doesn't give a damn what he looks like: easily told by the rags he is wearing.

- No. Your perfume.
- Oh it is just some local anti-perspirant I think it is funny they made it smell like perfume.
- I'm asking so many questions.
- Actually your questions are interesting.
- What did you study in university?

-       Business management. Didn't like it.

I feel he belongs in a creative field. But back in our planet and paradigm...

-       It's good, for a guy.
-       Maybe it is good, I'm just saying, I didn't like it. My dad was like, go study business, but I didn't choose it. Did you study university? I don't know what it's like in Russia.
-       I didn't study in Russia, I traveled a lot, lived in different countries, spent a while in the United States, actually I just came back from Miami. I have all these..
-       Oh my, were you in South Beach?!

He is interrupting, everything is hectic, rapid, the energy is a vortex. His hands are crossed behind his back as he is holding on to the pillar. Is he hiding? Or is he trying to ground himself because he is feeling the acceleration of energy we are producing??

He is wide open, his energy field is so rapid.

I stand closer to embrace his expanding aura.

-       I studied in California a while back, and I wanted to go to Stanford...
-       Really?
-       Yeah. But then some things changed. Then I was in Miami this year and I love it.
-       I don't know, I never been there. What do you like about it?
-       I love everything about it. I didn't go there for the parties though...
-       I didn't think so. I didn't think you went there for clubs or to hang out with Will Smith or Madonna. So what do you like about it?
-       Erhm just everything, the entourage, the shops, the restaurants, the ocean, the beach.

Ani Agata steps into the hall and we must all take our seats and then greet our teacher by standing up and waiting for her to sit down and then we all sit down. Like in court. All Rise.

...after the class we walk out of the meditation hall to get our afternoon tea.

- Would you like to share a chocolate?
- Hey...I was about to say that.

We sit down.

- Why are you here?
- I was going to go to the monastery and become a nun. I couldn't take living wanting things I couldn't have. There's a reason you can't have things you want.
- Yeah..
- And being in the States I couldn't find it either. And I thought...if I have to go to Nepal to find it, then I will.
- Yeah...
- How did you find the course?
- The people in India that I was teaching with told me. Right before the monastery I trekked to the Everest base camp. I have been traveling for a bit now. I really want to go further, probably Cambodia.
- I'm here for the course for 3 months which begins a few days after this course is over, I have been studying Buddhist teachings for a few years with an American teacher.
- Where have you traveled?
- I haven't traveled in Russia...only a couple of small cities outside Moscow...I went to visit my cousin who was getting married...but haven't met the girl before...
- He hadn't met the girl before the wedding?
- No...I mean...I haven't...they had been dating for two years. But...I didn't like her.
- Oh. So where have you been?
- The UK, Australia, Italy, Greece, the Caribbean...Uhm the United States...for a couple of months...right before coming here.
- Do you like it?
- Well...it's like, a place I become whole in, you know what I mean?

-   Yes.
-   It's just that at home, in Moscow, the energy of the people does not match, and it makes me feel worse. A lot of times I'm at home I want to be in the States, but then I realize the life is not for me, at times I think it is fake...
-   What religious background are you from?
-   Muslim.
-   Really? You can't tell...
-   Because I am not wearing a hijab?
-   I am Jewish.
-   I can't tell.
-   What do you do in Russia?
-   This actually calls for some more tea.

I pour some more of the yummy Nepalese milk tea.

-   I do a lot of spiritual work...Reiki...
-   I've had Reiki done to me once. A friend.
-   Yeah? Did it work?
-   She was in another state and she used a teddy bear.
-   Yeah that's what Diana Stein taught. Did you feel better?
-   I think yes. Where else have you been?
-   Spain, Prague..
-   I love Prague!
-   Me too. It is my favorite of all the European cities.
-   Have you been in Peru?
-   No.
-   You have to go. When you do, take the Inca Trail. I didn't go when I was there...cus my girlfriend...(cough) at the time, she didn't want to take the trail. So I should have taken the trek but we took the train. I should have just said, I will meet you there! She couldn't do it. But, I think, you could.
-   Yeah. How long have you been traveling for?
-   Four months.
-   Playing by ear?

-     Yes.
-     What are you doing next?
-     I'm going to Bhaktapur.

I grab his left hand and follow the Line of Destiny which turns into the Luna mount. The twist. Twist...twist of fate? His traveling. He was meant to travel and be out in the world.

-     Look, I have same line on my palm.
-     Wow, noone's ever read my palm before.

I see one line on the mount of Mercury indicating a loving partnership.

-     Are you only telling me the good things?

There's an attachment with someone..?

-     Have you been married?
-     No, no. I just need one...have you?
-     No.

We make our way to the dish washing kitchenette and rinse our cups.

-     Where do you get your eyes from? They're beautiful.
-     Where do you get yours?
-     My dad. My dad has blue eyes. Do you like yours?
-     Sometimes. I like yours.

...he starts to walk on as I notice he had left the tap on.

-     Are you going to leave the water on?
-     Oh. Yeah. No.
-
-     I don't think I will be going to the class. I feel a little sick. Sort of woozy.
-     Come.

...as we are sitting down in the meditation class, he takes his pillow and moves closer to me and sits on my left.

-     You didn't go to dinner, - as he shrugs and braces himself from shyness and excitement.
-     I'm just not hungry...
-     You will be hungry later.

- I don't like curry.
- Ha, you haven't spent time in India, you don't like curry. You get used to it.
- Oh. They gave us curry on the plane. Fish curry...ick....

All rise as the teacher walks in. We sit down and start chanting

Tayata Om Mune Mune Maha Munye Soha

...for 20 minutes, our minds go into different states, and from the intensity of the energies I had to move away from him.

Ani Agata tells us how it is said that soon after his enlightenment the Buddha passed a man on the road who was struck by the Buddha's extraordinary radiance and peaceful presence. The man stopped and asked, "My friend, what are you? Are you a celestial being or a god?"

"No," said the Buddha.

"Well, then, are you some kind of magician or wizard?" Again the Buddha answered, "No."

"Are you a man?"

"No."

"Well, my friend, then what are you?"

The Buddha replied, "I am awake."

Taking Refuge = Taking Exile = Ending the Program

- Are you okay? – asks Anson, as I walk out having put my prayer book down.
- Yeah...just a little nauseous. James!

At once he jumps up from leaning on the pillar. – You're all in it.

- I was just stretching!

We walk outside the Gompa. It's raining.

- Come on, come with me to my door. I'll give you my umbrella.
- Nah I'll be fine.

- How are you walking back? I don't want you to get sick. Come on.

We run to my door. He is tying his fisherman's pants up so they don't get wet.

- So you live here with the monks.
- I don't live with the monks.
- You're gonna be a nun.
- This is how you release, you just push this button.
- I can't take it. I'm gonna feel guilty tomorrow when you can't have it if it is raining.
- Just take it.
- Thank you.
- You're welcome.

I miss the meditation the next morning as I sleep in. I go to the class after my morning tea.

You will be trapped emotionally and physically until you learn to forgive and release.

Enlightenment is your ego's greatest disappointment

Proper preparation solves 80% of life's problems

If the sign on your heart says welcome, the love will come pouring in from everywhere.

A simple solution for finding a friend. Be yourself and see who shows up.

It doesn't make any difference what the surface behavior looks like. Underneath everyone wants to love and be loved.

You are creating it all...noone else doing it to you.

The more you give away the more you get back.

Ani Agata tells us how young people project themselves onto others and search for themselves in relationships. They fall in love first and then think the person of their affection is perfect and the only one out there for them and life makes no sense without them - but soon they realize that the person they fell for isn't what they thought they were. So they had a delusional perception of that person. Then they are hurt. They think they can't love another ever again. It is all delusions. We are not aware. We do not know how to love. One shouldn't stay focused on the one person, because there are so many out there.

Pleasure and pain. Pleasure becomes pain when that one object you enjoyed first, you can't enjoy anymore. Like laying out on the beach all day. You lay in the sun and then you want to swim, because you got hot. After you swim, you want to lay out in the sun again because you got cold. And it's a cycle. It is cyclic existence. Another class is over.

I have my lunch alone and walk out the canteen to the Gompa to take a picture. We are not supposed to talk until after lunchtime. I see James following me.

- Thank you. – he says, handing me the umbrella.
- You're welcome. – I whisper, and take a picture of the beautiful monastery building.
- I have been taking pictures too this morning. Just walking around.
- I want chocolate.
- Me too.
- I think the shop is closed though.

It will re-open in twenty minutes. We make our way past the library and past the Main Gompa as he tells me he used to smoke but can't anymore because of his head and his sinus problems.

- Do you need a medicine?
- Nah I'm fine, I got some proper ones...Oh wait no I'm not supposed to talk about my sinus problems.

As we approach the 1,000 Buddhas Relic Stupa - a place where all the Buddhas are abiding; a holy object of body, speech and mind - and a field for accumulating merit. Buddhists circumnavigate stupas and make offerings to the Buddha inside it. When nuns and monks pass by this one - they prostrate to it. This one is magical. If you make a wish, it will come true. James tells me how a monkey jumped on his shoulder and stole a banana from him when he visited the Monkey Temple - another name for Swayambhunath. He waves his hands in front of my face, which I find offending, but he does not realize it bothers me. I try and let it go.

We walk past a garden house. There are two paths – one leading to the garden house, and one leading back, out, to the shop.
-        I'm so going through changes.
We stood there, he wouldn't move. Something is stopping him.
-        Are you coming?
-        Actually....ahh...I wanted to get some chocolate. Shop must be open now.
I sit in the garden house. He talks to me, and then runs away to get chocolate or talk to friends.
I want to stay with him and exchange the energy with him.

I sit and contemplate. A kid monk is sleeping right next to me. We are in different worlds.

There is a Greek legend of Phaeton, who took his father's chariot but could not control it and had set the Universe on fire. Zeus had sent a thunderbolt to stop him from complete destruction. Phaeton was destroyed and so was the chariot. Sparse bits set as stars in the sky as the *Via Combusta* which one must walk in order to be re-born. The end of the road is November 21.

The smell of Nepali spices snaps me back to the present. I am sat at the canteen, my earphones in, looking out the window. He comes around, we smile at each other, he hands me a chocolate bar.

- I just kinda got caught up in the conversation. Sorry if you had been waiting.
- Well...you can do what you want...I guess...
- It's great I was just listening to some music too. Love it.

Students are sitting down for the discussion class. Anson isn't here.

- My roommate is asleep. Didn't feel like waking him up. Actually I missed the morning class. Can I see your notes?

Love and attachment are different.

Love - I want to share my happiness with others.

Attachment - I want you to make me happy. These things are opposite. Practice love and kindness. To be able to give love we have to have something to give first. It depends on training ourselves. Love is a state of mind. In the state of attachment, we develop pride, jealousy. Attachment arises out of ignorance. Ignorance projects a certain view of ourselves.

Love arises out of wisdom.

We reinforce our sense of things every time. If we like something, we want more of it, we reinforce it.

Attachment is always seeking pleasure, chasing it, but it never brings satisfaction.

Real happiness we have to develop within ourselves.

Pleasure is pleasure.

Happiness is an inner experience.

All pleasurable things have limitation. Happiness comes from cultivating the mind. The body has limitations. The mind has no limitations.

Attachment does not let us be in touch with reality. One way is to meditate on impermanence.

We need to make ourselves more in touch with reality.

As he flips through my notes I can feel the frustration from within me piling up.

- What she said really got to me. About pleasure and playing out on the beach.
- Why, 'cus you love the beach?
- Because she was right...it is never enough.
- Like, for me, I love cooking out in the sun. But when you swim in the ocean and then you get more sun you want to swim again and then again again...but then you want detachment and freedom. Like with a girl, for example, I believe when you are with someone, you should give them ALL of yourself. I know myself and now I can't do it, so I'm enjoying being alone.
- Hey, me too! – blurts out a fat girl in our group.
- I know it is so great to just be by yourself, hey! I love it!
That's it.
- You obviously sound like someone who's never known what love is.
- Huh...
- Well the only reason she told us things she did is because she doesn't have a man who cares for her. Does she have a man who cares for her? Does she have a man to make love to at night...
- She's a nun.

- Exactly my point. But don't take it personally. It is just...a sensitive subject.

James bites his nails. I take his hand out of his mouth slightly slapping it.

Ani Agata said there is time for sadness, but one must not dwell on someone they loved, when they are gone.

- Do you know what it's like to have someone and then SNAP! They're gone!
- That I just cannot comprehend. If you live with a person and love them for 10 years and then if they're gone you wouldn't even miss them? Like I know right now I am not in a position to start a relationship with someone simply because I believe you have to give them all of you and right now − I can't. At the same time I'd like to meet someone special...I just know that I always analyze situations and drive myself crazy.
- Do you think about that a lot?
- Yah if a friend at home, I mean I know this guy all my life, he loves me, but if he says something to me I would be eating myself up why he said that, why he looked at me in a way...
- Yeah...I know I used to do that for a long time. Then I thought to myself, I won't let you drive me crazy. I am a good person...I don't do shit to people...
- Yah. And I get jealous so much in relationships.

His vivid emotional body is reaching out with immense desire to learn and soak up new information. He has powerful spiritual connections but it hasn't been the time for him. He took off on this trip to find his answers. Strong feelings attract major spiritual powers. What if he is about to attract an important soul lesson? What if I am part of it? His need to learn and my need to teach can merge into a powerful time for both of us. Shall I talk to him? I want to ask him to come talk to me and say to him all I need to say to him. But what if he can't hear me. This has happened before. This is reminiscent.

At night I go outside the monastery to smoke with my newly made Danish friends. I believe they are staying in the same dormitory James is. It is behind the stupa. They say it's fun and cheap but very crowded in the communal bathroom in the morning. I am having second thoughts about the three month course ahead of me. I can't last the humidity for too long. I can't stay here knowing people out there are freely traveling all over the continent whereas I am locked up in the monastery. One of guys tells me about his experience with spirits and telekinesis. I ask him whether he feels stronger on his left side. He says yes. He also wears his bag on the right. His Spirit Guide stands on his left. He tells me how when he crosses the road he always only looks right...

...and his Spirit Guide watches out for his left.

We go back and past the Main Gompa where James is sat down chatting to a friend. He waves at me with both of his hands. Maybe he is waving at the Danish kids. We wave back and continue to walk on as I feel I just missed the opportune moment.

Next morning I wake up and before anyone gets in for the class I go inside the Gompa and open the Buddhist teachings book:

> **If you want to be appreciate, appreciate**
> **If you want to be touched, touch**
> **If you want to be loved, love**

> **What are you waiting for?**

We explore the Relic Museum underground one of the stupas. I see Lama Yeshe's preserved tooth. His ashes are kept within the monastery as well. Several ceremonial objects are for display. We are told about the musical instruments in Buddhism. Trumpets, horns and conch shells and other wind instruments have long been blown to dispel evil and to represent the sound of the Buddhist law. Particularly in Tibet, the trumpet is a very important part of the music that accompanies sacred ceremonies. They are usually made from bronze but in some cases from human or animal thigh bone. The far end of the trumpet is decorated with Buddhist motifs in silver and inlaid jewels. The sound of the conch shell - also one of the 8 auspicious symbols - has long been used in the Himalayas to call together a congregation. Its sound represents the spreading of the Law by the voice of the Buddha.

James looks absolutely cute in his windbreaker, absorbed by new education and a running mind.

I find Venerable Sven - the teacher of the 3-month course outside the Gompa and step up to introduce myself. I tell him I am wondering whether this is the right thing for me to do - to take the three month course, as I had planned for it but have other ideas right now. His eyes are looking down. He explains to me that a monk cannot look a person in the eyes. He tells me that if you take the course, that's okay. If you don't take the course, that's okay too. One must decide for themselves, and a monk cannot do it for them. I thank him for the advice and return to the Gompa to continue writing down important insights.

It is important to have a healthy ego

Self-confidence comes from the will power to help others

Lack of self-confidence, low self-esteem comes because we don't practice ethics. When we harm others, ill will, negative thought - even keeping it inside - churning inside of us - our self-esteem goes down. It is impossible to have a strong "I can do this".

Whereas looking at the bright side of life - gives us strength, confidence, as you choose to focus on the good.

When negative things take over - a person becomes depressed. Putting yourself into a mental disorder.

Start writing down the good things about life.

Mind will find more "Can do".

In a sense, this is a type of ego. But not ego-grasping.

During the class I am sending light onto James' emotional body. I can feel my thousand petal lotus opening as we chant our prayers.

The life of the Buddha is depicted on a thangka according to our textbook. During Buddha's 49 days of reaching enlightenment and sitting under the Boddhi tree, Mara, the God of Death and Destruction who was feeding on the sensual pleasures and the fear of death of human beings got very upset when Buddha had renounced physical pleasures. He sent three daughters of his named Desire, Fulfillment and Regret to manipulate Buddha in a vicious dance. He then tried to install fear in the Buddha's heart. But Buddha sat there settled and calm. And thus, Mara was defeated.

Buddhist believe in loving every sentient being as if they are our mothers. They believe that any insect could have been our mother in a past life – would we kill our mother?

We see not as the way they are, but the way we are.

Fill your life with experiences, not excuses.

Always do what is right. This will surprise some people and astonish the rest.

A marriage may be made in heaven but the maintenance is down here on Earth.

A person's true character is revealed by what he does when no-one is watching.

Success in marriage is more than finding the right person. It is becoming the right person.

- Are you my mother?! — James runs up to me on my right.
- Why...yes from now on, all sentient beings are to be treated like your mother.
-

We go to the dining hall and look out as the sun is setting down in the valley. It is gorgeous and it makes me want to embrace it in ways I can't because I am only human. But to feel the beauty of this. I feel like I am on a high. A high harmonic.

- I've always wanted to fly. Fly like a bird. You know?
- Well, go for it!

I shared my intimate memory with him and he made fun of it. I try and let it go.

Shall we sit together? Shall I put my plate down next to him? Why am I scared of him.

He puts his plate down first on *our* table. I put mine next to him.

- I'm worried about your cough.
- I'm fine I told you I took my medicine. You don't have to. You got your life to figure out. But thank you.
- I'm fine, I know what I'm doing. I got my head on my shoulders.
- Good. So do I.

I love how we play *challenger*. I move closer to him as I spotted a bug on his left shoulder. I am looking into his eyes. He isn't moving away. He must like me too.

- So what have you decided about your course?
- I just spoke to the teacher earlier. I don't know.

- Did you get some good vibes?
- Not really. I don't know. He is just sitting behind you. I was talking to him, he was not making eye contact with me...this guy is strange...
- Who? *This* guy? – as he points at himself.
- *This* guy has a thing or two that he won't tell....but I am talking about the one sitting behind you...
- Well you should figure it out, because as far as I can see a lot of this philosophy gets you mad.
- Philosophy doesn't get me mad!
- Oh, oh, I mean, THIS philosophy. And, its okay! Just...

...why is this such a guilt trip? Who was clingy and controlling in his family?

- I am either taking the course or not. It's as simple as that. I am also changing my mind about things.
- So what's the deal? Is it all or nothing?
- What do you mean?
- It's like, you either do it or you don't it. All or nothing.
- I am just not sure it's the right course any longer. A lot of things are changing in my spiritual world.
- So hey, can you see the aura?
- Sometimes. Or when I give a healing.
- Can you see mine?
- You have a strong bright red aura. It is jumping around.
- Yeah I can't get my thoughts together.
- Attention deficiency? Everybody in the US has attention deficiency.
- Well they don't REALLY have it.
- You know what gets me the most about being here?
- What.
- It is kind of personal but I will tell you. Couldn't I practice this in the real world. Did I have to come to the monastery to do it.
- Well there's nothing but getting more education from this.

Ignorance creates attachment, attachment creates anger. This is dependent arising.

If there is no ignorance, there is no samsara. it is the end.

Renunciation.

Ani Agata explains the meaning of the largest thangka in the Gompa - The Wheel of Cyclic Existence - the wheel of rebirth process is a graphic visual imagery symbolizing the modes of suffering endured by sentient beings of the six realms, along with the causes of suffering, which generate a perpetual cycle of rebirths. The wheel is firmly held in the teeth of the Raja - the Lord of Death. The four concentric rings comprise the entire wheel. The symbology of the twelve successive links of dependent origination resembles the twelve houses in astrology. A man being born, a man building a home, a man looking for a woman, a man giving in to sensual pleasures, a man and woman making a child, a man growing old and the wheel starts over again. The second inner circle represents the sufferings endured by the gods, antigods, humans, animals, tormented spirits and hell-bound beings in the six realms; the third ring indicates the dynamic rebirth process, and the innermost ring represents dependent arising: the pig represents ignorance leads to rooster represents attachment leads to snake represents anger...

In the top right corner Sakyamuni Buddha points the way out of the samsara - cycle of rebirth - pointing his arm to the scripture in Sanskrit - the Buddha language:

> Make effort to destroy it,
> Enter the Buddha Dharma, Eliminate the Lord of Death,
> Like an elephant destroys a grass-hut.
> Whoever takes up the practice of higher ethics
> With extreme conscientiousness
> Abandons the cycle of rebirth,
> And thus brings an end of suffering.

I will tell him everything. Everything about everything. Don't take it. *You see yourself with him — you were meant to take him there — you are given a chance — take it the way it is — he needs your guidance, but it will be solely your responsibility. . . .he will not be accessible. . . .you may either take it or drop it right now as this is the moment of the release of your soul.*

II. Higher ethics.

I came to the class early after walking in circles around the kitchen and canteen area. There was a notice board that one must sign up for washing dishes. Everyone had to do it at least once. James's name is already there. He was the first to sign up to help.

Delusion is a thought, emotion or impulse that is pervaded by ignorance, disturbs the mind, and initiates action (karma) which keeps one bound within cyclic existence.

Dharma - the teachings of a Buddha; the spiritual teachings and practices that protect one from suffering and lead to nirvana or full enlightenment.

Emptiness - the absence of the illusion of the inherent existence of people and things, upon realizing which one understands as ultimate truth.

Enlightenment - realization of truth achieved by an arhat (enemy destroyer - one who has overcome forces of karma and delusion and attained liberation from cyclic existence) and Buddha.

Ignorance - the root cause of cyclic existence; not knowing the way things actually are and misconstruing them to be permanent, satisfactory and inherently existent. the delusion that gives rise to all the delusions and the karma they motivate.

Imputation is the basic function of consciousness of giving a meaning to its objects. This meaning may not necessarily accord with what the object really is, a snake which is actually a coil of rope.

Equanimity - in meditation, a balanced state of mind upset by neither excitement nor sinking; as basis for compassion and love, an unbiased state of mind affect by neither attachment nor aversion towards others.

Karma - action; specifically those actions of the body, speech and mind, both wholesome and unwholesome, which are motivated by delusion and perpetuate the condition of cyclic existence through the process of moral causation.

Meditation - the process of controlling, training and transforming the mind that leads one to liberation and enlightenment. There are both analytical and concentrative forms of meditation.

Mental quiescence - the tranquil, single-pointed settling of the mind on an object of meditation for a sustained period of time.

Merit - the wholesome tendencies implanted in the mind as a result of skillful actions that ripen in the experience of happiness.

Nirvana - is the unconditional peace that is realized through becoming liberated from cyclic existence.

Penetrative insight - the meditative understanding of impermanence, selfless and emptiness that overcomes ignorance and leads to liberation.

Renunciation - the resolve to be liberated from cyclic existence.

Make you feel so right..
Whenever your body's laying next to mine
It's gonna get loose
Let's take it through the roof
Cause you know that you're the truth

Girl you're extra fine[1]

If one is used to very high things, then everything else becomes a problem.

Our mind creates seed which ripen at the time of death. They create the rebirth.

We do not have control over our rebirth.

If we are out of the samsara, we can choose.

I think about the time, I miss it greatly but the memory of us remains in my heart, recorded in our records of our lives.

Writing these lines just to remind myself how it used to be
The white beach. . .the swaying palms. . .
Just drive me. . .take me there. . .
In another circumstance I would have seen this differently. You know that better

Rinpoche - "precious" reincarnated lama.

Geshe - virtuous friend, spiritual friend who teaches Dharma.

Guru - interested and accepted to guide you. Significant teacher-disciple relationship.

The Buddhist path takes time - to check the teacher you found.

It is the ocean in which you need a navigator.

The last day of classes begins with a different topic. Ani Agata tells us a story about spirits staying in Tibet and enjoying the peace and calm. There was one girl who went to Tibet and got very sick with a rash

---

1   Lloyd, Feels So Right, alb. Southside

when she came back. There were no physiological reasons to explain the rash, but when she went to speak to a monk, he told her it is because she "went kaka" on a spirit while in the valleys of the Himalayas. They did a puja and it was gone.

She also tells us there are a lot of spirits around the monastery – and some people can see them. She asks if anyone has, and I see the gypsy girl nodding her head. She tells us you can only be attacked by a spirit – which has happened before to other students – if you have the karma to. Other people – sensitive people – can sense a presence in their room when they are alone.

It seems for the entire audience this is the most open and enjoyable discussion of all. It is what's on the agenda...and everyone's mind... the spirit world.

Ani Agata says that anyone who is ready to take refuge in the Three Precious Jewels - the Buddha, The Dharma and the Sangha - can do so with the presence of the Lama the last day of the course in the morning. In taking refuge, we oblige to follow the Buddha's path and not follow any other canon.

The night before everyone is leaving, energies come altogether into a bubble and mine was about to burst. I couldn't take being next to James without telling him I feel connection.

-        Hey. I just wanted to get some chocolate.

I approach him slowly as I see his legs shake as nervousness takes over him.

-        ...is this your personal time or.....

-        No, I'm actually just waiting for the library to open... reading *Siddhartha*...liking it. So what is it like outside the monastery? Is it all full of spirits?

...the calm in my heart...

-        Yes...they exist. Have you seen *Seven Years in Tibet*?

...my soft voice resonating from his body in a wave of emotion...

-       No, I haven't. What's it about? No, actually, don't tell me,
        or it won't be fun to watch. Where can I get it?
-       I've seen one at the monastery shop...and there's a DVD in
        the gompa...another good movie is *Little Buddha*...
-       So..how can we...when can we...watch it...I read it was
        inspired by when Lama Yeshe died twenty years ago and
        they recognized his reincarnation in a little Spanish boy
        and brought him to Kathmandu to live and study. He is
        no longer here though.

The library opens as I walk up the stairs and grab a book to read.
He follows me inside.

-       I can't believe I didn't come here before. It is so peaceful
        here.

Only Love Is Real by Brian Weiss for twenty minutes before we have
to meet at the discussion group. I walk to the session minute-to-minute.
He isn't there. He must be lost in the library. Anson and a tall strange
French guy are my company for this discussion group — they talk and
talk when I suddenly feel a bulge in my stomach as I am about to stand
up and leave. The discussion is about spirits and people's experiences —
they talk things one should keep to oneself. The spirit world does not
allow knowing of certain things. I never open up about my experiences.
That's just the rule. You keep it to yourself. Your Spirit. I will leave this
discussion class because it is boring without him. *Go. You will meet him at
the entrance.* I sit back and wait.

-       I had many experiences with spirits, - says Anson. I lived in
        Hawaii, and in the islands in the midst of the ocean, we're
        very dependent on the elements. People praise Gods of the
        Volcano, Wind, Rain and Fire. There was a place behind a
        rock in Maui, that a lot of people would jump from, for no
        apparent reason. As if an evil spirit was taking over them
        when they approached that area — and so I once tried to
        make an offering to it...

- Oh, when I traveling in Brazil I go to jungle and you know, indigenous peoples of Amazonas experiment much with ayahuasca – a plant, you know, for medicinal and spiritual purposes. I did and I really like. Very deep and spiritual.

Oh! There comes James. Thank God. I was about to leave. But hey, if I left I would have bumped into him on the way out. He comes into the group with a bag of goodies he got from the shop – sits down and maintains no eye contact with me.

- I've told about mine, what about you, James? – asks Anson.
- You must understand that for a Westerner there is no experience, it's very hard to get one.
- What about you, Djana?

I wondered whether I should tell them about the darkness and the attachment onto my energy body by an entity, and further having gone through extraction of it from my system that I experienced a year earlier. I decided in a matter like this, or this particular situation, I would feel too much of a drain had I started to pour out something so personal.

- I am just learning, - I said, as they kept muttering their own thing.

….he will never hear what I need to say to him. I will remain to myself. He is not making eye contact with me the entire discussion class.

- Well you didn't talk much today. – says Anson.
- Wasn't the right topic I guess.

I go back to my room and take a shower. I am sweating like a pig in this monsoons period. It is driving me crazy. I change into clean pants and put my shawl on. My hair is still wet as I go to the dinner. I missed on the afternoon class – I was doing my hand-washing.

I sit down at the canteen – at our place.

- Is it your personal time now, or?

-      No, you're good!

He puts his plate down. I am happy he is here. But what energy brought him? What is attracting him? What is the force behind our attraction? Is it affection? Is it time and experiment? Is it Buddhist memories and passages of lifetimes in exile and closed institutions. Is it political recourse? Have we been sent into exile? Is this why we are here?

-      I can't decide whether I should take the course or not.
-      Well you can stay a while and see, if you don't like it, you can leave.
-      That means I'm a cop-out.
-      Look, that's you making it up. That's you doing it. What do *you* want to do?
-      I want to go to Tibet.
-      There's plenty of overland trips to Lhasa.
-      That's not where I want to go anyway.
-      Where do you want to go?
-      Western Tibet.
-      What's that? Kailash?

How does he know of Kailash?

-      It's all over the tour agents. Many go there.
-      Ohhh...It's just that....I was in a different stage when I booked the course. I was in a different state. I paid the deposit so that nothing changes my mind and I don't change my plans.
-      Look you paid the deposit and that's a very noble thing. But you should see if you like it here, then stay and if not, just leave.
-      It is much more than that to me. Either I am taking the course or not. It's...all or nothing.
-      Look, I don't know you, but you can just follow your heart.

...another guy bums into our conversation.

-      Are you American?
-      I am Russian.

- You speak really good English.
- I studied in California.
- Where?
- In the Valley.
- I am from Southern California. Do you live there?
- No. After my language training I applied to a high school and was accepted but then realized no, this life is not for me. Seven years later...I almost applied to a university in Colorado to study Buddhism...
- Which one?
- Naropa University.
- I've heard of it.

James repossesses the conversation.

- She hates Americans.

Provocation.

- Really? Why? - asks the other guy.
- James said it...

He loves to get a reaction out of me.

- She uhm, signed up for the three-month course.

"She"? How impolite of him to say "she" in my *presence*.

I didn't say "he" in *his* presence!

I continue chewing on my chapati bread and local, monastery-made peanut butter.

- Peanut butter makes you happy.
- Fuck what my heart is saying. I have to stay with the course cus that's what I came here to do. Fuck my heart.
- Well...you should change your attitude.

I take my plate and stand up to take it to the washing.

- See you at the puja...

Why does he assume I am leaving?

I did not say goodbye. I am only going to wash my plate.

A puja is a ceremony in which prayers are offered to the Buddhas to draw down blessings or invoke their help. Pujas are performed to avert and clear obstacles, conditions which prevent humans from achieving their worldly and spiritual goals. In Russia Christian Orthodox cleansing with prayer and incense is a very common thing for a person as well as a house.

But...

...I am thinking to myself, I won't do it the "American" way. I won't act as I have before. As if I don't care – and try to pretend I wanna stay chill and be friends. We need so much time. But we don't have the time. And there are so many things that are so confusing about him. Some things don't fit together, he must be from another realm. Another life, parallel life, parallel reality...the future? Maybe. He is absorbed by staring at the monks chanting prayers.....I sat far away as I couldn't stay with him anymore but I did wait for him to come around.....and speak to me. But. He didn't. I was safe from now. But. Something causes me pain. I don't know what it is. Is it leaving this magical place? Is it feeling the emotions rise so high and the chants of the monks are so incredible. But so many things that are wrong about him. Too many things not fitting into place. His heritage. His birth in the US. Why do I feel like he's from somewhere else. Will he speak to me. Will he come to me tonight to share a time together before we part our ways?

<u>Next morning.</u>

There is a path of fear and the path of love.
Which will we follow?

The morning meditation is followed by saying our goodbyes and taking pictures. All students are getting their minds blessed with khatas – when offered and given back are considered protection. I stand in the back so noone can see me. James is getting his mind blessed. But he already has all the blessings. I can see, but he can't? He is searching for a spiritual experience.

Everyone goes to take a group picture by the stupa of I,000 Buddhas. James and I don't *speak*. I *think* of him constantly but I deliberately pissed him off so I am now free to walk my path and keep myself safe and integral. We seldom look at each other, thinking intwine, *Lets take a picture together.*

Everyone walks for lunch to the canteen. I sit and eat alone. Anka comes around to compromise a time to leave. We shall catch a cab to go to the tourist ghetto of Thamel. Her plan was to go to Tibet right after the course. Since a few days now, she has been pondering whether she should do the Green Tara retreat - which begins in a week. Otherwise she will go to Tibet. The Green Tara is the patron goddess of Tibet, a female deity and one of the 8 Taras who protect from fear, along with the White Tara - associated with longevity. However to do the retreat she would have to take refuge in the Buddha, the Dharma and the Sangha and not follow any other canon. She is not sure she wants to take it. I tell her if she does the retreat and it's not what she thought it would be, then she would have known she should have stuck with her initial plan and gone to Tibet.

James passes by me.

-        How are you today?

-        I'm fine.

He thinks I don't like him afterall. I watch him all the while as I sit with Anka and a guy from Tasmania and small talk.

-        I feel like talking to a Tarot card reader.

-        You're looking for guidance in other words, - says Tas.

-        I guess so. I just need a good answer whether to stay for the course or to follow my heart. Leave. That means my mind has no power over me, and I am used to following my mind when it comes to my carrier.

We chew on our lentils and rice. I hear James indistinctly in the background small-talking to Tina and laughing. I feel a mental connection. He is thinking about me too.

I go to my room and complete my packing. I floss my teeth from all the spices we had for lunch. Anka should be in the library. I better go check up on her, it is about time we leave. Taxi must be out and waiting. I am quickly walking through the pathway via the entrance to the library. Up the stairs.

- Djana! I just wanted to say bye.
- I *really* like you.
- Yeah I like you too.
- I think we may have been together in a previous lifetime cus I really feel a connection.
- Well I'm definitely drawn to you...obviously cus I keep walking after you every time...
- I'm feeling something I haven't felt in a looong time......my heart beats so fast....
- ...this is making me very nervous.
- I can feel my heart...it is beating so fast...it is going to jump out...
- Do you have e-mail?
- Yeah...
- Want to share it?
- Will you write? Cus if you do....my heart will start beating so fast...
- Well...how about...I will give you mine, so you can decide....
- Okay....Oooh...I'm too nervous to look for my book.
- I'm just a human being.
- You can say that...but I'm feeling something else...Gmail? This is for the US, right?
- Well, yeah, but everybody uses it. Want me to write down where you met me?

I wish he neared me and embraced me...my heart is drowning in the ocean of emotions.

- Your eyes are hypnotic...*you're* hypnotic.
- What are you doing after this?

- I'm going to Thamel.
- Yeah so are we.
- Where are you staying?
- Don't know.- shuddering.- We will meet at New Orleans café – you should come – the Danish guys will be there too.
- What time?
- Don't know. Maybe 9.

Surpass the relationship stage. Jump 2 break-up. End it, before it starts. He hurts me when I give him my world. I wait for him but he still does not know what we have. I make plans with him but he sabotages it.

- Okay I'll come. You're really something...

...standing against a wall cus I need something to hold on to before I fall. Already have.

- So what do you want to do?
- I don't know.
- Actually...I should go...now...people are waiting for me.....
- ...you're really.....something else.

We maintained eye-contact until he disappeared as he slowly walked down the stairs. I stood there for a minute to let the energy subside and sink within me and then walked up to the library. I am smiling to myself as I have chosen the path of love, and it is wonderful. So wonderful I am so happy I opened my heart truly. I released all my love onto him. His soul was shining at me and still connects to me – as I type this he speaks to me in my heart and soul.

III. The Road To Thamel.

At the top of a soaring emotion, flying like never before. My eyes shining, my lips smiling. I feel him all through me. Every tree and every cloud looking back at me and yearning towards me as I have just become one with nature as I have embraced loving another human being.

The receptionist of The Blue Horizon hotel greets us with *Namaste* = "I recognize the Buddha in you". The Buddha in me, meets the Buddha in *you*; while holding his hands in the *namaskara* mudra. Anka and I check into different rooms – I like to sleep alone. The room reflects me - it is spacious, with beautiful big windows and a big shower. The walls are blue. I feel so happy. I shower and change. I cover my shoulders with a white shawl and we make our way for lunch. I spot a gorgeous long blue skirt which makes me think of James. I have only but seen the first three dirt roads but I have just fallen in love and everything is shining back at me.

Oh so in love. Oh so blessed to finally be happily in love. Happily in love. In love...since...

The local women with crying babies in their arms aren't noticeable to me and neither are weird short men hissing "ganja" as we walk by. The dust of the streets and the noise of honking and tonking is not audible to me either.

...Angelic voices and praise in my heart and soul out-sound everything.

We go to an Internet Cafe which costs 50 US cents per hour. I check my e-mail to find a letter from Ani Inga - the registrar behind the three-month course. She tells me she understands how I feel about wanting to experience travel in Nepal instead of staying at the monastery. She was amazed by my strong intention to do this course in an authentic environment. She wants to encourage me to take the course for two weeks, and then decide whether I want to stay longer. The deposit is non-refundable. She thought it was such a good idea, that they are offering this opportunity to all the students enrolling.

I login to myspace and look him up. He lives in Hoboken, NJ. A profile picture from Iceland, looking hot. AND he is online right now. He is excited and he wants everyone waiting for him at home to know about it. I guess he is feeling a high as well. A chemical high we produce.

I also get an email from my sister, Amina. She is asking for my advice whether to go to Spain to do a summer language course or to stay for the entire season at home in Moscow. She wants to go, but she has doubts. I encourage her to follow her heart and take a chance on this course. Sometimes it is not what you want, but what you *don't* want, that carries you.

Anka had been encouraging me to talk about my frustration of the living conditions - the humidity during the monsoons period. She is used to it, but I am not. And the hygiene conditions bother me. Deep inside I know I am using it as an excuse for being bipolar and unable to be with my soul's mate, and this is the truth of all truths out there. And, the hygiene system.

...I try to keep my options open. I don't want to plan. Do I get attached to places, memories, people too quick? Maybe I just don't need a hundred years to know someone because I can see their soul. In their eyes. The first impression is the right one.

Anka decided to go to Tibet. We go to a travel agent a friend of hers recommended. All shops on Kantipath Road sell the same tour. *Numerous* souvenir shops, meditation classes, yoga classes, even Rei-ki, you can learn, by signing up. I never believe this...for a good reason.

The Green Hill Tours travel agent explains the 5-day drive-in and fly-out tour. It includes visiting monasteries in Gyantze and Xi-gatse, 3 days in Lhasa, visit to the former Palace of the Dalai Lama...

After relaxing at the hotel we go for dinner to New Orleans Cafe. I quietly hope James would come through to me, had everyone else been here by now. I just try to push it away. I want my space. I want my freedom. But I want *him* too. I ask Anka how she feels about relationships. She says she is friends with many of her ex-boyfriends. I think to myself, no wonder they are all ex's and they are friends - somebody like her is not something I would consider marriage material. It is her vibe, she doesn't want it, and she is not feminine or loving or kind. Having paid 250 rupees, plus a 50 rupees tip, we leave leave the restaurant. Anka says the waiters make about 600 rupees a day = 10 US dollars. So any tip is good. I tipped 20 %.

- Hey! Where you going! - one of the Danish guys from the course taps my shoulder on the way out of the restaurant. - Everyone is over there, come!
- It's okay, I don't want to go, I'm tired, - says Anka, - but you go, go.

I walk into the hall where everyone is sat down. James' eyes meet mine. It is the first time I see him without glasses. We smile at each other. I am walking towards him.

I am so glad you came.
...he catches himself drifting, pulls back to reality, looks away. Eye contact is lost.
I am lost.

I sit down in the first empty chair I see. No, I find myself a chair and sit down further away from him. The first empty chair was the chair right next to him.

Damn.

-       So why did you come to study Buddhism? – asked a chubby unattractive guy.

-       Because nothing else interested me. I've been through a lot and I was tired. There's nothing I want that this world can give me, but I felt comfortable in the world of Buddhism.

Do any other dialogues even matter when I have the object of my affection and desire right next to me. But I'm too shy to come to him.

He makes no eye contact with me. He is smoking and small-talking to a Dutch woman about the trip to Tibet. Ignoring the fact that I am here. I keep smoking nervously and having red wine glasses.

People start to leave and he stands up and cowardly passes by me – I hate it that he ignores me. What is he doing? Should I confront him? Should I leave? What the hell am I doing to do???

We walk outside on Kantipath. Something is familiar about this.

-       Do you want to smoke two?

-       No.

He is ahead of the entire group and I am walking behind him. Trying to understand.

This is reminiscent. Every moment.

He finds a café and everyone sits down. I try to be as close to him as possible.

This is the man I want. I want him and I will fight for him. I sit right next to him.

-       So what's new? What are you doing?

-       I'm going to Tibet. I'm excited! I'm looking at it as an education...

- What company you going with?
- Erhm, - starts searching in his bag, - it's called Tibet Tours…Look at me I'm flashing all these rupees…! - he pulls up his shirt to get his money belt as I notice the hair on his flat stomach. I am so checking him out.

Do you feel the energy flowing through you? Do you feel it? How can you know me so well? Can you understand my thoughts? Do you feel what I feel? This is a real gift…..And I've seen you how I dreamt of you before this meeting tonight. Before you are talking to me right now. Just like then…..a month later from this moment here. And over a year passed since. This rendezvous…..

- I can't take this. I really wannabe with you. – as I lean back in my seat.
- I've never had anyone…
- What? So straight-forward?
- Yes. Honest. I appreciate it. I do. And thank you. I wish I could reciprocate, but…
- No, don't say anything.
- Oh ok. It's like…I could kiss you but it wouldn't be the same.
- I wanna kiss you and touch you and be with you, wanna spend time with you, wanna get to know you better.

I rub his knee. For the first time he is wearing a sleeveless shirt.

- Now you don't have to cover your arms.

I put my hand gently on his beautiful face. He is so foreign. When he puts his mask on he is someone I never known. But I am here for a reason.

- Love…this is your year to find love.
- You mean…physical love?
- Love….there is nothing like it…it is what moves the world…there is only love in the world. This is the one thing that matters. Loving and being with that person. There is only two people in the world. Nobody else.
- Where….did you come from…you're like…the only Russian person I know…

…knocking on the door to his heart…….he just opened mine…

- I met you at the monastery and I feel you are very special. Don't ever let anyone convince you otherwise. And now I can't go back there as that place has become personal to me. I wish you could open your heart to love. You just need to open your heart. Would you open your heart to me?
- I wish I could reciprocate but…
- I want to spend time with you, get to know you, be next to you. I just…have so much love in my heart…and I need someone to give it to.
- So is this how you felt during the course?
- Yes.
- Why didn't you say anything? Or is this because girls and boys aren't really allowed near each other?
- Yes.
- What are you doing after this? Are you taking the course?
- Yes. Were you gonna ask me to come to Tibet with you?
- Yes. Well. I'd like for you to be *in my group*…but what if… things don't…Look I know myself.

…he is controlling it so well…a gift from the Stars belongs *there*, not here…another dimension. The dimension of light and endless, unconditional love.

- There is only love in this world. Only two people, and nobody else. When you are going to find that special someone who will treat you right…you are going to feel that much better. Cus you're a good man. And you will find your queen. You will. And you'll be her king.
- Huh. -smiles. – Do you think that person is you.
- I don't know. Only you can know that. I know you are special…and you will be happy in a relationship. And I didn't need to read your palm to know that.
- Are you always so open?

- No. I am introvert. I keep to myself. I just feel very comfortable with you.
- It's the first time you're smiling at me.
- I smile at you at the monastery.
- I really like it that you're so relaxed right now...I don't want to see you angry like last night.
- I know. Me neither. I'm relaxed because I'm next to you. Come on, you need a woman who's gonna stand with you. Support your aspirations and desires. Be the One for you.
- I seem to have problems I wasn't able to give all of myself to my last three girlfriends.
- Because you weren't made to wander around. You just need one, don't you. I feel it. I know you are pure. I know you've been through a lot....someone has done something to you...but you don't have to shut off...this is your time for love.
- I don't get it...how is it that you're so intuitive?
- It's just what I feel...
- It's a real gift!
- I just know things.
- Where did you come from!?

We embrace a little emotion and tears roll into our eyes.
The moment is enduring as is every moment with him.

"I hope you're happy. I hope I've said everything you wanted me to say. I hope it's over. It has to be. I need to get back to the course. I've done all I could. Let me go."

I take off, breaking tactile contact and run down the stairs out the door of the cafe.

I wake up and I can't take my mind off of him. This is madness but I need to get through this as he had left this morning and I will not meet him again. I am going to Swayambhunath. Dressing up, putting on my new beautiful blue skirt. It's about time. I take the rickshaw to the stupa. It is freaky in this town. I am walking towards the steps past Buddha statues and I am feeling pain. He is my mind. I feel the world coming down on me. The pain is so bad. I am connected to him on a one-way street and he is going to torture me. I can't believe this has happened again. This is so reminiscent of the past – and now it has happened again. Is there more I must say? I can't tell. I can't understand. All I know is it hurts so bad I am in tears and ladies selling jewelry keep asking me why am I so sad. Duh. I don't like turquoise or bracelets from selling ladies.

There are 365 steps to get to the stupa and is the only way pilgrims use, and the most memorable route for tourists to experience, so I go with it. I gasp trying to catch my breath, only to be stopped by a guard to pay 60 rupees for entry. There is a gigantic vajra - symbol of Tibetan Buddhism, placed on a plinth decorated with twelve animals of the Tibetan calendar. A smaller version of it would be a ceremonial tool in Tibetan Buddhism that symbolizes indestructible reality of buddhahood. It sometimes comes with a bell - making up a set of ritual implements, respectively symbolizing skillful means and discriminative awareness. There is a gigantic prayer wheel at the gate, which devotees spin to release prayers and mantras to heaven, and visitors are welcome to do so as well. Yes please.

I hear *Om Mani Padme Hum* playing distinctly in the background. It reminds the devotee of the Four Noble Truths. The lotus grows out of the mud to reveal its purity and beauty above water. Reciting the mantra helps the devotee rise above the imperfection and end the cycle of rebirths...

When the stupa was built 2,000 years ago, the Katmandu valley was filled with a great lake. According to a Buddhist legend, a single perfect lotus grew in the center of the lake. When the bodhisattva Manjushri drained the lake with a slash of his sword, the lotus flower settled on top of the hill and magically transformed into the stupa. Thus it is known as the Self-Created (Swayambhu) Stupa.

The whitewashed dome of the main stupa represents the womb of creation, with a phallic complement in the square tower. Rising from the tower is a spire made of 13 golden disks, representing the steps to enlightenment. The umbrella on top symbolizing enlightenment itself; some say it contains a bowl of precious stones.

The gigantic **Buddha eyes** gazing out sleepily from the *harmika* - the square section of the stupa above the dome from each side of the tower, oriented to the four cardinal directions, are those of the all-seeing Primordial Buddha. Between each pair of eyes is a symbol that looks like a question mark - the Nepali number "I" which represents the unity of all things. Gold plaques rising above the eyes like a crown depict the Five Dhyani Buddhas, celestial buddhas, associated with the five senses, the four cardinal directions plus the center, and many other symbolic groups of five - the transcendental Buddhas which exist in time and space...

I circumnavigate the stupa in clockwise direction, overlooking the entire Kathmandu Valley, and tears are rolling down my face, as I spin one prayer wheel after another. The Buddha eyes are so prevalent throughout the country that they have become a symbol of Nepal itself. I remember reading about the meaning and research of these gigantic eyes. I feel like *He* himself is watching me. The story of the evolved Atlanteans and Lemurians, connected with the samadhi state...as they are preserved, their vital organs functioning but their consciousness out *there*, they are hidden in the caves of Tibet for the benefit of all human race.

Humanity did not evolve, but degraded. Before we knew electric energy, kinetic energy, mechanical energy...there was only one form of energy. Psychic energy. It was culminated in the third eye - that which the Atlanteans used to build the pyramids. As humanity devolved, the third eye was blocked - for our own benefit as we had misused it. It was a measure of control.

I calm down. It might be psychically dirty here – the energy leftovers from rituals and people's emotions, and I might be too sensitive to them. Maybe it's best to just leave, now that I've seen it. I walk back to the hotel past women bathing their children and hand-washing their clothes in the river. A car drives by and into a pond as the dirt splashes all over my beautiful skirt.

Crying my eyes out, walking fast on the streets. There is no way I can find him here again. He is gone to Bhaktapur. I walk into the hotel and I know I need not be like in college – stay depressed, sit by myself, smoke. I need to find another agenda. I write a lot. Smoke a lot. Think a lot. Someone French. I walk down to the concierge to ask about getting to Patan. A guy named Vincent says he has a female friend who needs a companion to go places with. Would I like to meet her?

If only traveling was always so free. How can I be so happy and so depressed at the same time. Bipolar. My new friend, Cathy, takes me to visit Pashupatinath - The Temple of Living Beings - the oldest and holiest Hindu temple in all of Nepal. It is an important ritual bathing and cremation site, as the water in the nearby Bagmati River flows into the Ganges. It is said that if one is cremated here, they escape the cycle of rebirth. If a husband and wife bathe together in Pashupati they will find one another again, and be married, in their next lives. For centuries, women have committed *sati* here - throwing themselves into their husband's funeral pyres.

11 o'clock next morning. Cathy is nowhere to be found. I sit on the rooftop and smoke. I write in my diary the frequency highs and lows I feel. Priceless memory of love that has grown for him over the lifetimes we shared.

I am in this memory. I am somewhere else. I write. I sketch watchful eyes.
Something tells me I will meet him again today
...was a line I had written as my consciousness was nowhere to be found and my hand was practically writing itself. The eyes are all over the right page of my journal.

Cathy and I find each other and go to Patan by taxi and then to a French village of Lagangkel. We walk around the countryside and talk about astrology. Cathy's birthday is 21/11. Just about 11 years older than him. I didn't grasp this link at the time. Glitch of similarity – a similar numerological encoding – coming in to help me shift over the previous one.

We sit and smoke watching blue skies and duckies in the pond. We return to Thamel and sit on the balcony outside Cathy's room and smoke. We plan to go to Bhaktapur. Cathy has been traveling in India before she came to Nepal – she spent two months in Ladakh - a region in North India where the Tibetans live in exile. Among other towns in India that preserve the Tibetan cultural heritage are Dharamsala - where the Dalai Lama XIV lives when he is not traveling, and gives his yearly talk; and McLeod Ganj - Upper Dharamsala. She tells me she had seen a lot of people with distorted faces. She didn't realize it was because... when they fled from Tibet...they escaped through the Himalayan Range. The snow blizzard and the wind had been so strong...

She also says the most beautiful trekking scenery is in North India.

She puts some French moisturizing after-sun cream on my face as I had burnt and I am getting little freckles. I mean, come on, how much sun did I get. I am looking down from the balcony and I see him walking towards the hotel entrance. I let my hair loose. He leaves. I'm running after him down the stairs.

- Hey!
- Oh!
- What are you doing here?
- Just looking for a friend.
- Where are you going to? What are you doing?
- I'm going to Tibet...Saturday...
- Good, I'm happy for you.
- I'm not sure what I'm supposed to do right now...Invite you out, say, let's get some dinner, I don't want to lead you on to something and then you'll think it means something...and then spending time with me...your feelings for me will grow....

- That's my process. Don't worry...you can break my heart but it will heal itself.
- Oh I wouldn't want to —
- What are these?
- Mosquito bites.
- Do you need a spray? I have a spray...

I never use it.

- I have one...I just...never use it...I'm an idiot.
- ....I've been thinking about you.
- ...I've been thinking about you too...and what you've told me...
- Don't worry I won't give you a hard time. I won't stand in your way.
- ...and how you left. Abruptly.
- What was I supposed to do? Continue giving you a hard time!?
- Look, I can't give you anything right now. I think you're pretty...and...interesting...but I can't start anything right now...
- It's okay. It just means I'm not the One.
- Oh.
- It is the Saturn in your horoscope.
- You know astrology?
- Aha.
- You studied it by yourself?
- Aha.
- See...you're very...interesting.
- You should let me do your chart.
- I don't want to know the future.
- I know, I understand. I know exactly where you are.
- Metaphysically?
- How do you know metaphysics? No, I mean the stage you're in.
- See...not many girls can understand that.

- What's to understand? It's so simple when a guy is not in a stage to make an input into a relationship. I'm the same. I can't do it either. I think you're great, if you wanna be by yourself. I love that about you.
- Well that's what *you're* doing. That means *you're* great.
- Yeah...
- Yeah.
- I don't know, maybe you are one of those guys who wants to spend their lives by themselves, hanging out with pals. Alone. I mean how do I know.
- No, no...It's just that...I don't want to loose my freedom...
- What makes you think you would loose your freedom?
- We're traveling and...it is great to be by yourself....but it gets lonely...
- I know...
- You need someone...
- Well nobody needs anybody. We are born alone, we die alone.
- No, no!
- I mean, depends how you look at it!
- See I have been putting girls aside for a while.
- I know.
- Even then I couldn't give all of myself...my last three girl-friends...
- There's a wall around you...it needs to come down. Because love is the only thing that matters....Because souls... were created...as One. I can really feel it...something is wrong. Break it!
- It's my dad. He's just never gonna change. My therapist was even advocative of him. And it's taken me twenty five years...to work this....
- It takes a lifetime.
- I can't go home because he's there.
- But don't wait for him to change...

- I couldn't take his ways anymore, I was just like, I'm out of this, out of the family business. Can't do it anymore. I just spoke with him at home. Maybe if I continue talking it will all go into you.

I wiped it out of him as he spoke of his worry.

- I know what I'm doing.

I smile. He smiles back...and throws a small paper ball at me. I felt it break into my energy as our fields had been circulating in a powerful vortex.

- Why did you do that?
- Huh..?
- That hurt.
- Really?
- Yes. I felt it here, - touching myself at my throat, - and here, - and touching myself at my heart.
- I didn't mean to. I just woke up.
- We just came back from Patan. We also went to a French village.
- You went to Patan? I should have just gone with you. You just came back?
- Yeah.
- It's interesting. . ..I woke up and first thing I did was come here.

...he is wearing one of the silver-said-to-be bracelets with turquoise.

They are very...not *him*. Somebody gave it to him.

- Is this were you wear jewelry? Your right arm?
- Erhm. I don't know.
- Is it recent?
- Yeah. . ..this man in India gave it to me. I never wore jewelry before.
- You know what my brother told me about guys wearing jewelry on their right arm?

It is connected with the vision-center. It is in the left part of our heads. This means guys see on their left better than they do on their right. Thus they lean on the right side of their body onto a wall, to protect it as they can't see as well as they can with their left side. Or they hold their girlfriend on the right.

-       What was that your brother said?
-       It's like….see…men wear the marriage ring on the left, right? And women wear it on their right hand.

He is playing with my silver bracelet. – I like it. It's simple. I like simple things.

-       A lady in the US gave it to me for my birthday on the cruise. Pretty nice for someone you know for three days, hey.
-       It's nice. I like silver.

A local boy bums into our conversation, - Excuse me, sir, your bag is open.

-       Uh…huh? Nevermind.
-       Why don't you go and wash your hands first? And stop staring at my tits! - I spurt out.
-       Why you gotta be like that? You see, you get mad.
-       Well because he touched you!
-       You see! You're getting mad.
-       Does that make me a bad person?
-       No, doesn't make you a bad person! It's the little things! You get mad over little things!
-       No one has ever told me that…

Wow. He understands me too.

-       You know I love that you want to be by yourself and not create messes with relationships.
-       Yeah.
-       Because you know a lot of people look for themselves in relationships.
-       Huh? Who does that?
-       A lot of young people do.

- Well…you need to find yourself…
- Yeah it's more like when you find yourself is when you find your partner.
- Yeah. And I want to help people. But I really don't believe you can do before you help yourself.
- I agree. You know…I just feel it…you need so much love…I can't help it…I feel it.

…as I get woozy again.…the circulation around us has some sort of.…an intrusion.

I turn around.

I see a bum trying to break into my chakra of life-force.

- Look…Can we move 'cus this guy is breaking into my field.
- Yeah. Come on…I'll walk you back to the hotel. I've never been in love…you know…
- You've never been in love! How is this possible…
- I been with girls…
- Why were you even with them if you didn't love them?!
- Yeah…I always break up first with the girl.
- Ooooo…I see control issues…I saw you walking here with your head down so sad. Come on, cheer up, put your head up.

The tone of my voice and emotion intertwined within all the senses of loving him. I gently stroke his hair. Sensual and caring. He enjoys it. His face is drifting to a place of bliss. These moments are timeless and my heart becomes so heavy and bright.

- Shall we get some dinner?
- Aren't you leading me onto something?
- No…- as he rolled his eyes in a baby boy flirt-type way.
- Don't roll your eyes at me…Don't flirt with me. I'm not flirting with you.
- I'm not.…it's just the way I look…What do you want to eat?
- I want a fillet or a schnitzel.
- What's that?

- It's a chicken breast.
- Never heard anyone say that. I want meat, cus at the monastery we only ate rice and vegs. Do you mind if we find my friend first?
- Not at all. You looked so hot at the bar the other night.
- Ahem.

Why can't he feel what I feel.

- Okay, you weren't at the bar and you didn't look hot.

...we are passing on the main street of Kantipath past a paper lamp shop.

- I love these lamps. I already got some souvenirs and sent them home.

We make our way along to Hotel Utze. He asks for his friend as he comes down and they arrange to meet later.

- I bought these fisherman's pants, look.
- Why are they called fisherman pants?
- Because fishermen wear them I guess.

He says goodbye to his friend and we leave the hotel, turning around the corner

- Hold on, I wanna see these. I love crystals.

Nepal is the place to hunt for crystals and anything you ask the vendor as to "where is it from" is always from the Kathmandu Valley. Turquoise is everywhere – and when worn as a bracelet or ring – symbolizes safe journey for the traveler. Turquoise is a symbol of the blue of the sea and the sky. Infinity in the sky speaks of the limitless heights of ascension. The stone is opaque as the earth, yet it lifts the spirit high, laying bare the wisdom of the earth and the sky.

He stops at a wooden furniture shop.

- Do you like wooden furniture?
- Yes, I love it. Where is the place you wanted to go to?
- I...can't remember....I think it's further...
- Do guys stare at you a lot?
- Dunno.
- Well, I mean, here.

-    ...all the time...
-    It's because you're bright.
-    Ahem.
-    They all just want to sell you ganja.
-    I don't know, I haven't had anyone approach me.
-    That's strange.
-    Well, it takes guts to walk up to a lady.
-    They just approach everyone.

We walk up to the roof-top restaurant by the main square.

-    I like it.

I am so glad you do.

-    Did you choose the place by random?
-    Yes.

As we are sitting down, I suddenly feel his friends.

-    You hang out with your pals a lot at home, don't you?
-    Yeah sometimes.

He takes out his camera. I turn away.

-    Come on, I want to remember you.
-    You'll remember me.
-    It's sweet! Look!
-    Ah hate it! Look like a pornstar!
-    You don't look like a pornstar. You look cute. I'll keep it.
-    Yeah...put it up on myspace. "Hey, look at all the chicks I met."
-    Huh? Who does that? I'll e-mail it to you. Oh, I don't have your e-mail.

I just realized I didn't put my shields on when he took the picture. I was bare and I felt fine.

We get the menu. I light my last cigarette. He takes out an anti-septic gel and hands it over to me.

-    Did you eat here before?
-    Nope. I ate at another place.
-    You didn't....?
-    Huh?

- You didn't….?
- What??
- Didn't make you sick?
- No.
- Okay good. You never know what they give you here.

The waiter comes to take our order.

- I'd have a chicken schnitzel with mashed potatoes and a glass of red wine.

He ducks his head down again.

- I'll have a burrito and a beer.

I am picking up different things. It slows down as I am able to distinguish.

- Do you wear contacts?
- Sometimes. Normally. But in the monastery I was like, nah, who cares. You?
- I wear contacts too.
- Who do you look like?
- My grandmother.
- You're very pretty.
- Thank you.
- I don't know, different people tell me, I look like my mom, or my dad, or both.

He starts to bite his nails again. Is he manic? Is he obsessive-compulsive?

I type this and find myself biting my own nails. Dang.

- Stop it. I'm going to hold your hand so you stop biting your nails.

He smiles. He loves it. He loves it that I know what he needs.

- What do you eat at home?
- I have to have chicken at least once a day for lunch or dinner. I love mashed potatoes.
- I know I love mashed potatoes.
- Never eat pigs or porks.
- Why not?

- Cus you are what you eat.
- Hmmm never looked at it that way.

Our food arrives.

- I've seen your pictures from India.
- Really? Where?
- Myspace.
- Really? You found me?
- Yeah. Your profile catch says, *Namaste, bitches.*
- Yeah so.
- Funny. biAtches.
- Nah it didn't say biAtches.
- But there weren't any pictures of yourself.
- Yeah there were some. You know, I can understand not using a Western toilet, but I can't understand not using toilet paper.
- Hahaha. There are still toilets in Moscow like that, haha. Man. Like in the center of the city with designer stores but still old squat toilets. There are Russians sitting behind us. They are swearing like pigs. Pigs!
- Can I ask how old you are?
- Yes, you can.
- How old are you?
- How old do you think I am?
- Ah don't ask that question. I hate that question. Okay, based on what you've told me, not how you look...

...his eyes were so big and watery...

- I would say...28-29?
- I am 22.
- No you're not.
- I don't lie...I was born in '85.

Pause.

- So how come...you...
- I've been...through...a lot....depression. Tremendous... pain...

- By yourself or other people?
- Other people.
- You're very intelligent. You're 22. You know what it's like in the US? The age people graduate they don't know *what* to do in their lives. You're 22 and you've done so much.
- Could have done a lot more.
- How could you do all these things by 22?
- What do you mean.
- You need time to do them. So what has...driven you here...?

...memory flushed over me and my eyes reflected pain.

This second time had paused. Again.

- Did I make you feel bad? – he said as he noticed me go into a trance.
- No, - I take a sip of red wine, -...I did.
- Have you read *The Celestine Prophecy*?
- No.
- Read it...
- Okay.
- You know I've never seen eyes like yours....I mean I have seen blue eyes...but yours...are clear...
- It is my soul shining at you.
- Yeah you can definitely tell a lot from a person's eyes. What kind of background do you come from?
- I am the oldest of three, I have a brother and a sister. I love my family. They've given me everything. And we've taught each other so much. My parents have told me many times I've taught *them* a lot.
- Yeah, they didn't know *what* to do with us.
- Do you have a sister?
- Brother. Younger.
- What is your mother like?
- She is a beautiful, caring and wonderful mom, she still looks like she is 30. It's...my father...who is difficult. And

nobody gets it. Everybody loves him. Like, if you met him, you would love him. I just don't want to work under his patronage anymore.

- What does he do?
- Construction.
- It's good. Have you heard of this movie *What the bleep do we know?!*
- I've heard of it.
- It's about quantum physics and quantum reality.
- Aha…
- I can't give you a definition…
- I wasn't thinking you would.
- You know places like the monastery and metaphysical institutions attract all kinds of people…weird people…trust me on this.
- Oh yeah, like that French guy with ayahuasca in the discussion group!
- Yeah!
- See you know what? It's so difficult to just relax and unwind and give in.
- Very easy.

…when you're in love…

- Nahh. See, people like us – are worse cus we think too much. We analyze too much.
- Well…it's good cus you're hard on yourself…
- Ignorance is bliss…

He pulls out two incense sticks from his bag.

- I lit some of these and walked around the Boudhanath yesterday. Do you *smoke?*
- No.
- I like to sometimes. There's a place…we can go there later.

We finish our food.

- What are you thinking?
- I so want a cigarette…

He calls up the waiter and asks him for a cigarette and hands it over to me.

- What are *you* thinking?
- Just enjoying my company.

We pay our bill and leave the restaurant.

- I need to get some cash.
- There's an ATM. Come I'll show you.

I get my cash. He is not there. I stand and wait. Can't psyche. Time is stopping. Dropping? Cutting off. I can't tell. He waves at me as I look at a souvenir shop across the street.

- Which one do you like?
- This. – as I point at a square-shaped ashtray he is holding in his left hand deciding which one to get: this one or the hexagonal one, in his right hand.
- Do you know where is the Meditation Center?
- It is right there. I don't know if this is a good idea, but we can go to Bhaktapur tomorrow.
- I *am* going to Bhaktapur tomorrow.
- Cool. I want to go to the morning meditation, and class. I don't think I'll be going to the dance. Let's meet here at 10.
- Okay. In case something changes, I'm waiting for you for 15 minutes and then I'm leaving.
- Okay.

He disappears. I can't believe it. He wants carnal pleasures of nargyle and smoking hash. I won't do it with him. This is not what we are here for. I walk down the street to my hotel and realize I need to get smokes. I walk back to the square and see him rushing somewhere. I think he might have come early and his friend wasn't there. His quick walk. His biting his nails again. His mind. It is running. Attention deficiency. Hyperactivity.

I wake up late. I missed the class. I get ready, seeing us going to Bhaktapur. Cathy and I go for some breakfast as I rush seeing time ahead of me – can I make it there on time? It's 10:10 a.m. He is not here.

-       Cathy, come I'll show you something. They have dance and
        yoga classes.
We walk to the Meditation Center.
*Maybe there's way too many issues within you I will never understand. Maybe
loving you is my part of my journey all by myself which you will never embrace with me
as I have seen us in dreamtime.*

-       There you are!
-       Actually I only came because you gave me very strict rules.
        I just woke up.
-       Are you ready to go?
-       No.
-       Okay...well. We're going...yeah.
-       Okay...I'll meet you there...If I go! - as he disappears be-
        hind the gate of the Meditation Center.

Bhaktapur means "The City of Devotees" in Pali and is renowned
for its art, culture and festivals, historical monuments and craft works,
pottery and weaving industries, temples, ponds, rich local customs and
musical mystic. Bhaktapur is still an untouched as well as preserved ancient city, and is itself a world to explore. I keep looking out for him. I
want to see him. But he is never there. I feel watched. It must be the eyes
of the Buddha. *Go back.* We make our way through a little passage to exit
from the entrance. It begins to rain! Oh no! My pink espadrilles! We
run into the first open shop – the Thangka painting school.

I see one thangka that resembles the cosmos = it is a circle...with
three divides....on a blue background....soon we will be reconciled to
that blue source. Those who are awakened, will retain the memory of
this experience and move over. Those who aren't will be sent back never
knowing what had hit them. Only locals are allowed to learn the art of
thangka painting. Cathy is talking to the salesman.

Created at a higher dimensional level of thought and consciousness, our souls will be reconciled back to the source by the fastest mov-

ing frequency color = blue. Our entire bodies respond to the vibration of that color immediately - it opens our communicative and psychic abilities. When you find yourself being drawn to the color blue, it means your soul is awakening and stirring. Follow that drawing. It is your Soul, *calling*.

We are trapped in the shop and it won't stop raining. I mentally dissolve in the paintings around me. The rain stops and we make our way out. I am very conscious. Very aware. Absent-mindedness has turned into mindful awareness. I feel like a little princess, wearing this beautiful skirt that reflects the psychic energy of the color blue and reaches out to him even stronger, enhancing my ability to stay with him.

Cathy and I come back to the hotel. I wander around the streets *very* blue. Never meet him. Our minds stop our hearts from reaching out – and we do not meet. Our program is embedded in the grid in a way that we do not go about randomly, but always within the game.

IV. Lam Rim

Everyone has a path to walk, imprints brought into life in order to experience and complete karma. The chemical structure of the brain put in order to produce certain afflictions to experience our path.

Past the illusion. . .look past. . .beyond the physical appearance. . .I am looking at you.

NOW
His memory has been wiped out, erased

I hear your voice, I see your face in my mind
Your eyes driving me
Taking me there, beyond the dimensions
It's just what I know

I have returned to the monastery and checked in. I have all my sheets and clean towels, and I am prepared to do this for the next three months.

"I am thinking about your eyes, your smile...I miss talking to you, looking at you and feeling the good energy coming from you. Thank you for showing up, and making mine a pleasant experience. Just looking in your eyes and being next to you was so pleasing.

I hope you enjoy Tibet and make it a learning experience. I feel there will be a spiritual shift for you when you are there, and you will discover new things about yourself and move to a new level of experience.

Wherever your path shall take you, I am thinking for you and hoping that you let yourself take things nice an easy; relax, sit back and enjoy your unique experience, and let things come to you.

You're special, remember."

I press send and read it over and over five times until I get up and walk to my dorm. I meet a girl named Adrienne, whom I find extremely interesting. She reminds me of someone. Everything here seems so different without him. It is like it is dead. Everything that mattered is gone. He is gone.

Adrienne introduces me to a friend of hers, Simon, from New Zealand. He likes to take photographs, easily told by his professional SLR. I meet Ani Inga in her office.
- Hi! It is so nice to finally meet you!
- So nice to meet you too!
- How have you been?
- Good. I am here to get the handouts for the class, it is starting in a few minutes.
- Yes, here they are. Check them. And you are clear about the enrollment conditions?
- Yes, I understand, two weeks, and then decide. That works for me!

I walk to the classroom.
- Namaskar! I got the materials!

We each get a Dharma Book Cover and Pocket to keep our study materials together. Students introduce themselves. Maybe if I can control the way sounds come out of my mouth I can manipulate my mood. If I speak slow and sweet, my mood will become slow and sweet.

This basic program is about the Lam Rim – the Stages of the Path.

With study comes understanding; but this must be put to use. It is therefore vital to put as much as one can of what one has studied into practice...

The real wish for complete enlightenment can be only altruistic, as for all sentient beings. This motivation is developed on the stage of higher meditation.

The wish to attain liberation is motivation. From the karma point of view, you get only what you wish for. So one must identify properly what is it, and then wish for it.

To give up happiness of this life - doesn't mean to give away possessions. It's more about change of attitude other than change of circumstances. It is to give up grasping and clinging of this life. Which makes impossible to enjoy life, as one gets upset when one can't get what one wants. When the happiness of this life finishes, it is like trying to keep a snowflake in a matchbox.

I don't think I can do this for three months. Adrienne is going to Thamel as we have our first day off the next day after the course begins. She books her tour to Tibet and we stroll to the crystal shop. I buy a pink quartz crystal. We were supposed to see the lama in the morning but I came to the Gompa early and felt a sudden churn in my stomach which signalled to me that I should leave. I haven't always followed this reaction of my body. As we are leaving the monastery I can feel a change of the future. While he is in transit to Lhasa and I am here – it all depends on where I go. It's a resonation. It's a pull of two polarities – where he goes, I go. Where I go, he goes.

Mind and Mental Factors, says the handout. It outlines the 3 poisons and secondary delusions. Ignorance, attachment, hatred. Ignorance leads to dullness, laziness, inattentiveness, concealment, faithlessness and forgetfulness. Attachment leads to avarice, self-satisfaction and excitement. Together ignorance and attachment lead to dishonesty and pretension. Hatred leads to wrath, spite, cruelty, vengeance and envy. Together the 3 poisons give birth to inconsideration, unconscientiousness, shamelessness and distraction.

The six root afflictions. An affliction – is an awareness that causes the mental continuum to be very unpeaceful when it arises. For example, attachment is a mental factor that perceives a contaminated thing to be attractive by way of its own entity and thereupon seeks it. Its function is to produce suffering. The antidote is to mediate on contentment. Ignorance is a mental factor of unknowing that is obscured regarding the mode of abiding of all phenomena. Its function is acting as a support for the arising of wrong ascertainment, doubt and afflictions with respect to phenomena. The antidote is wisdom of realizing selflessness.

There are 51 mental factors. There are 5 omnipresent factors, 5 determining factors, virtuous factors, root afflictions, secondary afflictions. Intention – moves and directs the mind that accompanies it to its object. It has the function of engaging the mind in the virtuous, non-virtuous, and neutral. Intention is the most important of all mental factors because through its power minds and mental factors engage in objects. Mindfulness is non-forgetfulness with respect to a familiar phenomenon. It has the function of causing non-distraction.

On an afternoon off, Adrienne and I sit outside the dormitory. She has powerful spiritual connections. She reminds me a lot of Nicolette, my soul=sister and confidant, powerful karmic and soul connection in the "right after college" window. She and I traveled in Cyprus, where I lived at the time, visited many pranic healing workshops and initiated many places with our presence, connected by an ancient legend going back to Isis, hence our desire to travel together to Egypt on a cruise, which never happened as both of us relied on the Universe to lead us having thus missed out on the fact that all cruises are suspended during winter...she talked to the Angels and guided me on my way. Adrienne reads cards too. I am trying to persuade her to read mine. She has 5 tiny gemstones on her window sill, they were given to her by a Peruvian shaman. I normally don't like to touch other people's belongings... especially rocks that contain energy and memory...energetic blueprint... but she hands me an obsidian as I get dizzy and hand it over back to her. How could James trigger me to be so psychically powerful. How can this be possible. She hands me a clear quartz crystal which makes me feel a lot better. It is very powerful. It even has a water bubble inside. It is unique.

I read psychology: the difference between love and co-dependence. Every word confirms my true love. I am so deeply in love. So glaring at the skies and wishing for him to come back, as this is my next vision – he is coming back here to study with me and do this course together as One and grow on our paths. He will appear at this gate, when my Soul appears before *him* and instructs him to come <u>here.</u>

There is an interesting woman right across from me. A nun. She is wonderful and another past life memory hits me...

The four noble truths have four aspects. True sufferings – mental and physical aggregates produced by contaminated actions and afflictions are:

Impermanent because of being produced occasionally and not existing forever (counters viewing them as permanent).

Miserable because of being under the control of the contaminated actions and afflictions (counter viewing them as pure and pleasurable).

Empty because of being devoid of a supervisory self that is a different entity from them (counters viewing true suffering as a self).

Selfless because of not existing as an independent self but being under the influence of many other impermanent factors (counters the viewing of them as a self-sufficient person or as the objects of use of such a person).

The beautiful nun smiles at me as we make eye contact. She reminds me of someone. She has beautiful shoulders and facial bone structure. Her name is Ani Jen.

...how am I going to last three months. This is torture. The mountains are calling for me.

Unrealistic thinking – either positively exaggerates the positive objects or exaggerates the negative aspects. In the first case it leads to attachment and in the second to anger.

I hear so many voices and write so many things, draw his chart as I am trying to understand him, I am having visions of his future – the timeline and the lifetime. I am seeing the past. At times I get confused. I can't make it out. It is hard to focus with so many people around me. I constantly need to be by myself. Why was I holding his hand? What happened and who did it? Was it my holding his hand? Had I been a channel? Had a connection happened? Had an attachment begun? A string maybe? "If she held your hand and told you things….she was an empath." I understand. This is it. I had been an empath and my gift has finally shown itself as it is meant to function.

If you have a good self view – my life is alright or I am alright. There are different types of happiness. Sensory happiness – depends on sensory power. Mental happiness – depends on mental power. Bliss in meditation is mental consciousness. We are sense-oriented. It's not easy to realize our mental consciousness.

I stand outside the dining hall waiting for our food. Ani Jen approaches me.

- Hi, I saw you in the classroom, we smiled at each other but I don't know your name.
- I am Djana.
- Interesting...who gave you that name?
- My mother.
- Where are you from?
- Moscow.
- Interesting...do you know what your name means?
- No...
- It means "knowledge" in Sanskrit.

The morning meditation brings me to him. I see him right in front of me, telling me something. He is saying, come with me. *Follow me.* I have to follow him to Tibet.

Sang gyacho dang sog kyi chog nam la
Jang chub bar du dag ni kyab su chi
Dag gi jin sog gyi pa tsog nam kyi
Dro la pen chir sang gye drub par shog

At the time of non-attachment, the mind is quite happy. Then you see the object of attachment. Then one thinks one is unhappy because it doesn't have the object of attachment. But how does mind generate attachment? The appearance of aspect of attachment is greatly exaggerated by unrealistic thinking. To the point where your life seems meaningless without the object. E.g. advertisement pushing the things we really desire, one is freedom. The mind gets caught up in that. Another one is power – buy the car and become very powerful.

Some things are a mental creation – the more, the stranger it appears. Then it becomes "I must have this". The sad thing is, we actually make decisions based on these states of mind – we desire something that is completely ordinary – unimportant.

We make decisions that have an incredible impact on our lives.

Free the mind of mental afflictions and liberate ourselves are two goals of Buddha's teachings.

We have to work with unrealistic thought, primarily. To go from an object is usually not an option for most people. Sometimes people do retreat – get away from the object. The mind gets a new view of the object. The way to counteract unrealistic thinking is to generate antidotes in the mind.

Come in analytical meditation. E.g. anger is a distorted state of mind. When angry, it is hard to see any quality in the person. One has to meditate on the kindness of the other sentient beings. A good antidote is to remind oneself that the other person is under the influence of the affliction too. And does not know of it.

One is able to counteract one's mental afflictions. Sometimes it takes time so then there are also relapses. It is similar to overcome addiction. It helps to remind oneself that one's mind is impermanent and does not exist on one's side. Because of the strong grasping and permanence, and side existence.

Fatalistic attitude comes. And one thinks he can't change it. It is a mistake in attitude – as one CAN change one's mind. Need to understand the antidotes and apply them. Sometimes they are simpler than one thinks.

During an audience, I ask Ani Jen why she became a nun. She says....extreme...pain.

Classes are long. Our teacher, Venerable Sven barely makes eye contact with the students and I am hardly listening; drawing lotus flowers in my sketchbook. "How do I take control of this gift? I must be by myself. I must return home. I cannot remain here. The course isn't going to work. My delusional mind is in love – I can't take anything else. I must leave in order to shift this attachment. It has to happen. I must go. Please let me go."

According to the Dharma, the Buddha explained that consciousness is a clear and knowing phenomenon with certain other characteristics, such as being a creature of habit, and always being accompanied by a subtle psychic energy.

The "clear" refers to the mind's ability to reflect objects and eliminates the mind as matter, i.e. something atomically based. It can also refer to the intrinsically pure nature of the mind. This clear nature of the mind is something only to be seen in meditation when the disturbing thoughts have subsided. At that time the clear nature of the mind can shine through. But even for normal people the mind is usually clearer in the morning than later in the day. Why is that? By confirming that our mind has this clear nature we have confirmed one essential feature the Buddha attributed to mind.

That our consciousness is a creature of habit we can easily verify for ourselves. We only need to observe our consciousness for a few days or weeks to see that it follows established patterns, which confirms another characteristic that the Buddha attributed to mind.

The Buddha also taught that consciousness always goes hand in hand with a psychic energy that acts as its vehicle, and that these energies travel in a network of psychic channels in our body. By controlling these energies one is able to control ones mind. Both these psychic energies as well as the channels are subtle types of form, not recognizable with the eye.

Explanations regarding these psychic energies and psychic channels can also be found in Chinese medicine, where the energy is referred to as "chi", and Indian yoga, where it is referred to as "prana". Quite often students of these disciplines can see the relationship between consciousness and energy through their own experience. Opening blockages in certain channels, so that energies can flow freely, brings also mental relief. Directing the energy to certain parts within one's body heightens the awareness there. These are small personal experiences through which one can confirm that the teaching of the Buddha on the corelationship of consciousness and the subtle energy that acts as its vehicle is true.

Having arrived at the understanding that consciousness is the clear and knowing entity described by the Buddha we then have to contemplate on its impermanence. While we might not be able to see immediately its subtle momentary nature, we can certainly observe its coarse impermanence. How often changes our mind in the course of the day? How many thoughts come and go in the course of a minute? These obvious changes in the mind would not be possible if the mind was not momentary and since it is momentary it has causes and conditions.

One of the girls on the course is from Hungary, at breakfast she asks me about the Russian way of drinking tea. I tell her, I drink tea with chocolate. She says, no, no, no. Russians drink tea from a samovar, a big pot for brewing tea (literally self-brew = samo-var) and full of preserved berries and fruit. Right. She is talking about *vareniye* - a preserve of berries with sugar, dissolved in the tea, thereby invigorating it with vitamins. Her boyfriend tells me he saw me dancing on the rooftop by the clothes hangers. Busted! He says it looked like a mix of yoga with dance and stretching. That is exactly what I was doing. The girl asks if I was actually doing exercise? Her boyfriend says yes. He says I am doing it right now. She says, *how? Raising the toast?!*

They had been traveling for a while. They met online back in Hungary through a mutual interest in Buddhism and meditation. They had been together for five years. They had been doing retreats, traveling Asia and practicing Dharma. She seems very mature and I am quite comfortable with her. It sounds like James and I could do the same thing. When I ask her how she makes a living, she tells me she rents out her apartment in Bucharest which is enough for them to live in India or Pakistan or Nepal and when they need additional money they sell local souvenirs and craftwork to their friends back home.

Another friend I make is Luis from Chile. He has amazing eyes. He is short, very well-read, has a lot to share and is very passionate about Buddhism. He also travels solo, and has just come from India on a motorbike. When he bought it, he did a puja for it. I connect with him. Our conversation is easy, I tell him that I want to leave, I have to go to Tibet, other places, I want to travel the entire South and Central American continents. He has been to most places, particularly Belize, which was amazing - San Pedro *is* La Isla Bonita. He tells me it is not safe for me to travel in that area by myself. He tells me if I do go, I should go to Easter Island. He tells me about the crystals he had found in the Chilean Andes which were enormous and I feel this connection...a lucid dream I had a while back...of my other half traveling to the mountains to find a rock, and keeping it until we reunite. Minerals have tremendous power. Combined with very clear and strong intention and a psychically powerful place - they are able to attract energies beyond imagination. We were minerals in our past lives.....like asteroids, from outer space. From different planets. I feel an enormous connection from my second center of life force when I think of outer space rocks. I feel in a different reality I might be experiencing as a mineral. As for right now, the energy of the pink crystal is enhancing my kindness and I am so loving, these energies within my body are changing my consciousness and I feel things I've never felt before. How could I be at the monastery and in love.

You're the One I give my heart to
As I'm the One who loves you so much
You're my inspiration
Cant wait to see your face again
Cant wait for you to come here
And stay with me
Cant wait for this time

I know I'll be here waiting
One day, that day
I seen it in my dreams
I'll see you there and I'll know
I'm doing it, with you

I buy a postcard of my favorite Buddhist art images, the Samant-abhadra - the male aspect of primordial buddha-body of actual reality - he is blue in color and symbolizes luminosity. He is sitting in lotus position with Samantabhadri in his arms facing him - the female counterpart symbolizing emptiness. A total union = as the two most important forces in the Universe are wisdom and compassion according to Buddhist philosophy. They must both be present for harmony to exist in the universe and for enlightenment to be possible.

A connection so deep and incredible
Amazing I know you could feel me

I dream about him. I hold my pink crystal and invigorate it with the energy of the deepest love I have ever known. I keep going to the stairs of the library and remembering the times....those few minutes that time had stopped and there was us. We can have the world at our feet. Isn't this what you dreamed of? Haven't you been wanting this.

> Having been sent to you to guard you
> I feel I will always do this
> I just want to hold you in my arms
> Feel you heart beat
> Listen to your breath
> Feel your skin touch on mine
> Feel your warmth

I wear my blue skirt every time the connection is stronger. I wake up after a nap and see him rolling in the sheets with me and whispering words of love and eternal truth as we are now together and nothing else comes close.

I day-dream about trekking to Mt. Kailash and camping at Lake Manasarovar. If the mythical utopian kingdom of Shambhala is some-where in the valleys of Tibet, Mt. Kailash is the manifestation of the mythical mountain of Meru - it is a sacred peak of over 6,000 meters. It is regarded by Buddhists, Hindus and Jains and followers of other spiri-tual traditions as the 'heart of the world' as its geographical positioning as the watershed of South Asia is unique and gives it a cosmic geomantic power. From its slopes, flow four great rivers in the four cardinal direc-tions - the Indus North, the Brahmaputra East, the Karnali South into the Ganges and the Sutlej West.

The Hungarian girl, Ditti, tells me she had been to Kailash as they sneaked into Western Tibet from Pakistan and it was amazing - she had seen it from all the four sides and the North Face is the most beautiful. It is seen as a snow-capped pyramid. The living conditions were *shit* and she hated it. People would do their needs out in the streets, squatting and putting their long *chubas* down. Once she did her business and all the *shit* went up as the wind was blowing from underneath the hole in the squat "toilet".

Apparently we are expecting one American guy to join the course. I don't understand how it is possible...because the advertisement for the three-month course outlined very specifically that ONLY those who have taken the introductory course can enroll into this three-month course.

We get almost two full days off. We go to Thamel to an airline office as I need to find out if I change my ticket to fly out earlier than planned if I can't take the course anymore. It seems I won't be since I found it. Right? If I had to fly out I would fly out without going about looking for tickets and comparing prices. The fact that the line is two hours of a wait and I suspect they won't be able to change my ticket as I bought it with an agent and not with the airline, I realize I can get a refund from STA when I return to Moscow with a different flight. We go to another airline office to ask for prices. It is a 500-something dollar one-way ticket. We return to the monastery and I take a picture of the skies setting down it is beautiful how much I wish you were here. *I set myself up to fall in love with the man who left.*

If I can take this pain with me – then I will be safe from new pain, whispers my mind. If this writing will be carried on to the United States mainland it will be found and connected to where it is meant to find its belonging. As you will. But you must be prepared. Listen carefully to the messages. Observe the metaphors. Meditate and watch. Listen. Twelve around One.

We go to visit the Osho Tabopan and I have a reading.
Higher Realms, let be channeled the information I need.

Release – Ending – Adventure. In the past you release something. Something is coming to its completion right now.

The future is an unpredictable adventure.

We walk from Thamel to Durbar Square - which means "Palace" and it is where the kings of Nepal are crowned. There are fifty statues, temples and monuments along with monkeys, goats and hundreds of pigeons, *sadhus* - holy men - begging for money, local vendors selling garlands of marigolds and fruit, along with souvenir stalls. It reminds me of a Middle-Eastern market with all the sacks of grains and spices. I find a woman selling rock salt. Just like the Himalayan salt lamp I bought for my father's birthday before I left home. I know of their protective properties. They are sold by weight. I buy five pieces.

We had been told that begging is a problem in Nepal. Some parents encourage their children to dress in rags and beg tourists for money after school. I decide not to encourage this practice and thus do not give any money out. It would only reinforce the cyclical nature of poverty and dependence upon Western generosity. And how long can you be saving someone, until you are forever responsible for saving them?

We are about to leave the taxi square as...I see one of the guys from our introductory course. I wonder if James is nearby as my heart is beating so loud that I barely hear my own thoughts.
- Hey!
- Oh, hi!
- What's up? What have you been doing?
- I just came back from Tibet. It was awesome. The flight back was expensive. We had a great time. Actually you know some guys from our group.

No shit.
- Oh yeah? Who?
- Well, James went, - my heart is jumping out, - and the Danish kids...and this other Dutch woman.
- What Dutch woman?
- Well you know she was with us in the group.

- Don't know.
- Oh come on, the one who owns The Last Resort.
- Oh. Well I am taking the three-month course.

If you see James tell him I love him!!!

- Well that's enthusiastic!
- Actually we do have to go now, so...
- Yeah, nice talking to you! – as he shakes my hand, I realize I don't even know his name.

We take a taxi back to the monastery. He is constantly on my mind. I am suffering. Is he back in Nepal? "No. He remains and is taking his journey further from there." I take a shower and change and go upstairs to the rooftop to do my stretching. It is wonderful and watching the mountains and feeling him all throughout my being and being in love with him is what I choose. Did I just enroll to take refuge? And quickly found myself an excuse to quit. The Q. The Q is the Quit. It is the Quest. The Quest he is taking as I am taking the Quit. Escape button.

I put four rock salts around the four corners underneath my bed and one on the window sill.

He must be out of my mind by tomorrow. I do my hand-washing. I do my cleaning duties as I have taken up the task of washing the toilets. Why do I feel watched and monitored?? Why do I feel he is everything I need to be and everyone else is only trying to convince me my path is wrong and to remain here and keep soaking up the energy of this place which now makes no sense to me – the only thing that does – is my mad love for James.

- I bought some rock salts today, Luis.
- Oh wow what are you going to do, black magic and hard-core sorcery?!

Why do I feel like I'm dying inside...dying because I'm so into love and so want to give and share myself with the world but you're all I can ever hear in my heart and mind. You're the beauty in my life that lightens up my days. My smile goes out to you. I want to sing whenever I think of you.

You're all I want to know, ever
Cus since you've showed me
I always know

…another day begins with the scent of juniper incense – and calm abiding meditation. Quietly I sneak into the meditation hall as everyone is already there. And off we go. Visions of him again. And again. And more peanut butter with bread for breakfast and milk tea, which makes my belly rumble. I hope it doesn't rumble too loud to make my classmates not be able to focus.

There are seven types of awareness. They are direct perception, inferential cognizer, subsequent cognizer, correct assumption, awareness to which the object appears but is not ascertained, doubt, wrong consciousness. Direct perception - non-mistaken knower that is free from conceptuality. Needs to have a focal condition of the object. There are four kinds of direct perception. Sense direct perception, mental direct perception, self-knowing direct perception and yogi-direct perception.

Conceptual consciousness is always mistaken, but not necessarily wrong. The clear knowing is preceded by consciousness. Eye sense power makes it sense consciousness. Blue causes it to have the aspect of blue.

It is important to distinguish mental consciousness and sense consciousness. They do not really have any power. Sense consciousness is very unstable. The significance of the external object cannot be overstated. Only by focusing on the internal object that negative thoughts can be pacified. Primarily engaged thoughts engage external objects - they really bother the mind.

Also sense consciousness of the object is very coarse. Cannot perceive very subtle. Not suitable for analytical meditation. From the point of view of meditation. The root of our problems lies in the mental consciousness. What is happening in the mental consciousness far outweighs what is happening in the sense consciousness.

We meditate on the reflection of the outer object - in our mind. If something is an object of prime cognition, it exists. If not, then it doesn't. Just because an object appears - believed in, makes it true. Even if all sentient beings were to believe one thing, it would not necessarily make it true. The object has to be rooted in reality. Prime cognition to impermanence, emptiness, liberation. To become enlightened, one has to generate prime cognition with regards to the path - the Buddha, the Dharma, the Sangha.

Also one must generate inferential cognition of the objects. There are parallels to the principle for human emotions. For every negative emotion there is an exactly opposite positive emotion. Emotions that create opposing frequencies: hate-gratitude, anger-kindness, fear-courage, anxiety-peace of mind, pressure-presence of mind.

It is three days until the two weeks expire. I see Ven. Sven walking my way.
- Venerable Sven? Is that you? Can we talk? I really need to talk.
- Yes, yes.

We circle the stupa just like James and I did. Sven asks me how do I find the course. I tell him it is interesting and he is also driven by my enthusiasm and strong intention but
- I am going through...an emotional....thing....I need to get rid of...
- What is that emotional thing exactly....
- Well...I met a guy....
- ...you will meet someone else.
- Buddhism really doesn't believe in the One does it?
- No...because if he was the one for you, he would have been here, with you.

- Yeah..
- You will find somebody else.
- I don't want anybody else.
- Your mind is not clear.

It is so difficult to have a power and not be able to control it.

It could take you years of patterning relationships doing the same thing all over and over again.

Let me caress you
Let me take care of you
Let your wall come down
Let my love come shining in

If you can't control something, it controls you.

If you did not resist this, but let my love come shining, filling in the space that's yearning for it you know it would be so great if me and you...you know? And you'll know when it's right, you'll want to guard and protect. You'll want to keep that image in your mind, no matter what. You were made to be happy and you know it. It's because I'm feeling this with you.

The salt has leaked out of the rocks and made a gross mess under my bed. At night I lay without sleep till six in the morning and then drift to a beautiful place having decided that I cannot stay here any longer – the anguish will eventually drive me and now it's over – I won't let it drive me any crazier than I have already driven myself. I won't fight – someone has just shown me that I cannot remain here. I'm leaving Nepal. I'm returning home. I need to be by myself. But first I must finish all the things that I can do here. Tibet.

- Would you really think they would give up material life? - I hear indistinct conversation.
- No, but I want to plant the seed.

My heart is my carrier now. I am excited and so in love - and I know in a moment or so my love will be right next to me. Nothing matters and I choose love. I choose you. I chose to feel you and go wherever you are *calling* me. I am letting go. I am giving in to you.

* * *

I book Tibet with Green Hill Tours, but it is still a week away. I have all this time in Kathmandu. I hope he comes back and stays at the Meditation Center. But the place just felt so wrong. I can hardly rest and I make no friends. I decided to go back to The Bluue Horizon. I go to the Weizin Bakery to have hot chocolate.

...love and urge to be with him no matter all the predictions, no matter the prognosis or outcome.

I have searched online about empathy energy and found a book called *Dancers Between Realms*. I'm glad I left the course, I needed freedom. Had I had more money for this trip I would have done things differently. When I left Moscow I left my check card. I have good money saved for the trip of my lifetime, and I did not take it because I wanted to travel with the little bit of money and I had enough to cover the course expenses. I will return home, it was pre-planned, by my Higher Self. But right now...my mind is clouded. I can't think. I can't project. I can't plan. Need to get my ticket. Tried a few agencies but somehow it never works. Should I get a date, what date? Should I leave Nepal on the 17 or 19 of July? Can't tell. I need just enough time to create the energy to help me make the transition away from here. Someone else should come into my life before I leave Nepal. I decide to go on the 14th. I call the airline and make a booking. I go to their office and they input my credit card number and expiration date. They realize they had just misspelled my name and need to make a new booking. I leave because I am mad at them for this big blow and try a travel agent. A rep swipes my card and tells me it is rejected. I go mad. I go online. I check my account. There was a charge of five hundred something dollars made. I can't see who made it. I am going nuts. I call the bank in Moscow. They won't tell me. I yell at the girl in the call center. Resultless. I figure it has to be the airline as they are the only ones who input my card info this morning. I go back to their office and the woman who entered my card number for the booking with the wrong name denies her mistake as I yell at her for this stupidity and sabotage. I go back to the hotel. I call dad. I tell him what happened. He sends me the money I need for the ticket. I go and book it from an agent right next to my hotel. I have chosen to leave on the 14th. I have paid for the ticket and now a-waiting for things to settle. For my heart and mind to find compromise. Please...

"He might not recognize you when you have finally met again, even though you know him. you can see the potential, the future; but he does not. His fears, his intellect, his problems keep a veil over his heart's eyes. He does not let you help him sweep the veil aside. You mourn and grieve, and he moves on. Destiny can be so delicate.

You may be awakened to the presence of your soul companion by a look, a dream, a memory, a feeling...you may be awakened by the touch of his hands, and your soul is jolted back to life."[2]

You will see me in the crowd...and you will recognize your-self.

A soulmate who is available but unawakened happens to be a tragic figure which can cause great anguish. Unawakened in a sense of not seeing life clearly, not being aware of the many levels of existence. Everyday mind prevents awakening.

As the vibrational energy of spirit is slowed down so that denser environments such as third-dimension can be experienced, the effect is for the spirit to crystallize and transform into denser bodies. The densest of all is the physical body, and the vibrational rate is the slowest. Time appears faster in this state because it is inversely related to the vibrational rate. As the vibrational rate is increased = time slows down.

On my way from the café to the hotel a blonde girl approaches me, saying a friend of hers is writing a book and would like to interview me.

- What do you do?
- Reiki, astrology...
- Really? What is your ascendant?
- Aquarius.
- Very good! I do cards, you know.
- Can you read mine?
- I think yes! How about this, I read your cards, and you buy me a drink.
- Sure.
- What has been the best thing during your trip?
- Meeting a wonderful man.
- Well, of course! How many men have you dated?
- It's irrelevant.
- How many men have you had sex with?
- Haha.
- Okay let's do your cards now. Think of a question.

She lays three cards down leaving the 4th card facing down.

- Got your question?
- Yes.

She opens the 4th card.

- Oh! Can't have the reading now. It's not the time. The energy is blocked.
- I see.
- But, maybe you should have the reading some other time.

I see a simple cotton bias-cut grey dress from afar in one of the numerous clothing stores. I buy it for 200 rupees. It is about four dollars. I walk to the hotel and see a jewelry store that's open for another few minutes before closing for lunch. I explore beautiful silver bracelets and symbols.

"Love is the ultimate answer and it is not an abstraction, but an energy = spectrum of energies, which one can "create" and maintain in their being. One begins to touch God within oneself when one is feeling love.

Love dissolves fear. One cannot be afraid when one is feeling love. If everything is energy and love encompasses all energies = all is love. It is a strong clue to the nature of God. When one is loving and unafraid, one can forgive. The hardest thing is to forgive oneself. One forgives oneself, and then others. One sees with the right perspective. Guilt and anger are reflections of fear. Guilt is a subtle anger directed inward. Forgiveness dissolves guilt and anger. They are unnecessary, damaging emotions. Forgive. This is an act of love.

Pride might get in the way of forgiving. It is a manifestation of ego. Ego is the transient, false self. One is not their ego. One is greater than all of these, one needs their ego to survive in the three-dimensional world, but one only needs the part of ego which processes information. The rest - pride, arrogance, defensiveness, fear - is worse than useless. Ego separates one from wisdom, joy and God. One must transcend their ego and find their true self. The true self is the permanent, deepest part. It is the wise, loving, safe and joyful."

I go to the roof-top restaurant. We must share our knowledge with other people...We all have abilities far beyond what we use. We develop through relationships. There are some with higher powers who have come back with more knowledge. They will seek out those who need the development and help them.

...you are the One who triggered so much more and helped me realize so much more that learning in the spiritual state is much faster, much more accelerated from learning in the physical state. But it is we who choose what we need to learn. If we need to come back to work through a relationship, we come back. if we are finished with it, then we go on. In spiritual form one can always contact those in the physical state. But only if there is importance there...if one has to tell them something they must know.

Sometimes one can appear before that person...and look the same way one did when they were here. Other times one just makes a mental contact. The messages are most probably cryptic, but most often one knows what it pertains to. It is mind-to-mind contact.

I develop my film and the photo of me at the gateway
to Bhaktapur has his essence all over it. I am shining.

"It is safe to love completely, without holding back. You can never be truly rejected. It is only when the ego is involved that we feel bruised and vulnerable. Love itself is absolute and all-encompassing. The concept of loving completely and without reservation may seem risky or even dangerous. This is not about self-abrogation on a relationship or enduring a relationship that is abusive or damaging. Doing so is not loving to yourself or to the other. Staying in a destructive relationship is not an example of loving without reservation - instead it may be more a manifestation of low self-esteem and lack of self-love than anything else."[3]

...a clarity in my mind has settled...as a song was playing in the background
I love the way you dream, I love the way you dream[4]...

-        Knock, knock! Your bus is here!
It's early morning...and I barely prepared...after a sleepless night. I am only taking a day pack and 2 plastic bags of toilet paper and water for the trip. It sounds like there is gonna be drought.

---

3   Ditto
4   Buddha Bar, *I love the way you dream* by One Giant Leap

I leave my suitcase at the hotel's storage room to come back in 9 days.

I am the last one to hop on the bus.

-        Hi, I'm Etienne! I'm from Montréal.

Cute guy with blue eyes.

V. Tibet

*D*ay 1. It will take 5 days to get to Lhasa by the Friendship highway. We are driving to the border to complete immigration formalities. I'm only but following his spirit. Would he be the patron of my traveling?

> …sheet of paper along the way…just write it down. Quietly. …
> *Maybe in that other life you remember me…*
> *You remember*
> *Me and you and how we used to be*
> *My heart and my love forever yours*

We make a stop for coffee. My group includes two Dutch girls, a girl from Bulgaria, with whom I have a strong *deja vu*, two women from Macedonia, a French man who lives in Tahiti, a few American kids and a Mexican guy. The Nepalese guide explains to us that the bus will drop us off at the border from where we will walk to immigration and then take a jeep for the entire week with a Tibetan tour guide. There are a total of 10 jeeps, tours run every Tuesday and Saturday, so the immigration officials are prepared for our group, and everyone is working "by-a-clock" so-to-speak. After coffee, we take off. I try not to smoke. We drive through the jungle, I see waterfalls, stupas, rivers, in the midst of dream-like scenery. You can go river-rafting here. The bus makes a stop for us to buy some water. Hey, it won't be drought after-all!

The Last Resort is the last stop before the border-town of Kodari - I like the symbolism of it. The bungy jump is here, among other extreme activities. Etienne and I walk the bridge over a mountain river gorge. I look down and start panicking as Etienne tries to be as supportive as he can. He takes a picture for me. I could never do a bungy jump. I am scared of heights. We walk back to the bus and I snatch a cigarette from one of the Macedonian women.

We arrive at Kodari and line up to get stamped out of Nepal at the immigration "office". They tell me that when I return, I can get a *visa gratis* for 14 days. We walk to the Chinese border with our bags. Local kids try making some money working as porters. I refuse it. Etienne asks me what do I do and I tell him I just finished a course in Kathmandu and I work as a translator and he tells me he did a degree in Marketing and I say I did as well. I did a Sociology program with a major in PR, Marketing and Advertising, which I think is all bullshit, or, more precisely, the wrong energy for me. He asks me if so, then why did I even do it. I told him I did not chose it. He asks me if this was a guy thing. I tell him my friends were going to apply that day and so I went and applied with them. Which is not entirely true, as my sister and my mom encouraged me to apply and I was accepted. The line to the Chinese immigration is preceded by a line to supposedly check our blood pressure. There is another line, for locals, traders and smugglers, whose blood pressure is not checked. But we tourists, we have to go through it, apparently for our good? We walk to immigration to be stamped into China. When I picked up my passport the day before, the agent told me not to bring any Dalai Lama pictures or books against the Chinese government. Neither is there a sticker visa in my passport - which I miss because I want to have all pages filled up. I am used to having paperwork in order. If there is no visa in my passport, where is evidence I actually have been to this country?!

But hey, this is a Special Tibet Travel Permit. It is a piece of paper with Chinese writing on it and two words in English: my name. The immigration officials are very strict. Five peoples' passports have been just taken and walked away with into a locked dark room for verification and brought back after twenty minutes. I fear if this is what is going to happen to me. I always do, ever since I traveled to the States last year -

and was sent for additional screening because the customs guy did not like that my passport was new - and all pages were empty - there was only one visa. I was interrogated for three hours. It cost me missing my plane, getting to Boulder super-late, five hours of hopelessly trying to calm down and an eye inflammation.

I hand my passport over with my permit. The official stamps the permit and gives me back the documents, no problem. I am happy and at ease. It's raining outside and we hide in the den. I see the Bulgarian girl. She looks like an aspect of me. A me a few years ago. Somehow, her energy reads close. Her background maybe? Her name is Lila. She is traveling solo as she works in Chennai, India for a translation company, she is project manager. Surprise, surprise! I tell her I am a beauty therapist. I just haven't worked in that career for years. I want to own a salon.

Two other girls in the den with us are from Holland. They look like two lesbian hippies. They are, alright. They are exhibiting their artwork when they return to Kathmandu. I tell them that if I come, I will be super quick, as that is how I am - if I like something, I stay, if not, I leave. We get in our jeep. Lila, the two Dutch girls and I. Etienne wanted to be in the same jeep as me. I did, as well. It is a fun, harmless flirtation. But he will distract me. I don't need that. The jeep takes us to the hotel - a dormitory, as we had been warned, with no shower. A bathroom will be a whole in the floor. Bring your own toilet paper!

It rains as we go to eat Chinese food at a restaurant downstairs. I order sweet and sour chicken for 15 Yuan. It is roughly 2 dollars. But it is gross and after barely munching on the white rice I return to the dorm. I walk in the hall. I feel I want to stay here. With him. I saw this in my mind - we meet in the hallway. Two paths, walking toward one another, the fantasy is real. I pick a bed, tuck in and try to stay warm in my sleeping bag but I can't sleep. I wonder if he slept in this same bed. I wonder if he, just as I, couldn't sleep in this bed. Otherwise I wouldn't have chosen it. It is right next to the big window as I like my bed and with a view of the mountains. I breathe on the glass of the window and draw a heart on it...

One day, some day, we reunite
I'll be yours and you'll be mine
As we were meant to be
Forever one, like we are, as we are

Day 2. It is barely dawn and we have to take off. We've a lot to drive. We make a stop in Nyalam after two hours through the jungle before dawn and having breakfast. It is amazing what deprivation of enough food, proper sleep and shower can do. Now we are eating eggs and Tibetan bread. And drinking my soon-to-become favorite: yak tea. And here comes the sun. And we take off. As I realize I left my sunglasses in the dormitory the night before.

OMMMMMM

All these years you have been
And remain my only real truth
You're the one I was created with and forever in my heart I am carrying you. I want you baby I love you as I always have in my soul, truly and deeply. You're the One that makes me complete. You're my second half.

My heart is wishing you open yours to mine and let my love in
I love you. . .I love

We stop for photos and we can see the Everest - the highest point on the Earth's continental crust, at 8,848 meters. In Russia this mountain is known as Zhomolungma - its Tibetan name which means Mother Goddess of the Universe. It is breathtaking. I take photos. We stop over for lunch in one of the rest-aurants on the highway. The rest-area is also a hole in the ground. But these are actually much healthier for your body. Squat, not sit.

I have a black tea with sugar for lunch, and, bummer, a cigarette. It is all I wanted, really.

They say acclimatization to the altitude change and deprivation of oxygen can be tough. I believe....we are used to dirt polluted air we breathe in the city and once we go out into a place as clean as the zero point field of Tibet - our convolutions are filled with the virgin oxygen from the mountains and the heavens...and our brains are chemically changed and mystical things happen. They also say that once you have been so high up, any lesser altitude change would not affect you.

Every look, every mountain, takes me high up to cloud number nine. The piano keys are lingering in my soul.. ..as I am listening to the notes of A minor played in my mp3. I'm tired of false pretenses. . .I have found somebody for real.. ...I know you felt it too. It's just that we are in different worlds and nothing is ever changing this. You are from another world, reality, timeline, we can't be. We were never meant to meet. But we did. It's the karma for me I have created and driven myself mad and to the edge. The journey since I have taken the path to study Buddhism, since Naropa University, I have experienced heights and lows, but always with you. And then I came up so high and decided to change the energies and take my journey all the way to Nepal, and booking the course the last day I was in Mia.

...I think I dozed off to some different place...what is happening I don't know...

We just arrived somewhere...I think it's Gyantze.

I feel awful. I can't hold myself. What am I feeling. Vomiting? Sick? Dizzy?

-   It's the altitude, hun. We just crossed over 3,000 miles up and down in one day. Everyone is sick now.

I think I'm about to drop down and shift elsewhere. Why do I feel like I will die in this place. Am I dying and waking up to a different reality? I can't take this. I am about to drop dead.

-   Okay now! Get a grip, it's going to be okay. Don't worry you have altitude sickness you will be alright. Martina here is studying to be a doctor and she will know what to do.

He is so hectic. American. Do all Americans have attention deficiency? Are they trying to balance their hecticness? Are they ill? Are they mere normal human beings with a lot of energy and I am just mad in this place.

-          Hey! What are you feeling?

Martina. Such a beautiful couple. They're so in love. Matt is from Maui in Hawaii. Tanned, slim, blue-eyed and dark-haired. And so reminiscent of James. Why aren't we here together. Why do both mess up our lives. Couldn't we be here together. Why is my love wasted.

The town – or a stopover village on the highway is called Lhatse and we are getting comfortable. There is no shower. Tomorrow we are in Xigatse, and will have a proper hotel. And THEN I can wash my hair.

I want to see you happy and content. The path you've chosen is not easy but it shows you've courage. I really care about you. Want you to know this. Travel safe and be good. One day you'll know what it feels like to be devoted to One. The One and only. You

One of the English girls insists I drink some electrolyte balancing powder drink and eat. I am not hungry. Definitely don't want to eat. I go back to the dorm. I am sleeping next to the window. I lay down. I pray for Love. Truth. Clarity.

Please save me. Don't let me die.

How we experience an event – it is the result of karma.

I want to be there with him...in this world I drift to...when my physical body is giving up.

Day 3. I wake up and feel fresh as a cucumber, and light as rain. I thank heavens for sparing me. I slept the night. We are driving to Xigatse, the second biggest city in Tibet.

There are so many things I want to tell you. I wish I could hold your hand and look into your eyes one more time, feeling the bliss I felt when I did. And I wondered if there was a place in time that belongs to us and I had loved you dearly. I wish I could share the peace I felt being in the mountains with you, feeling your energy, feeling you close to me, standing next to me. I wish the time had been for us to embrace this harmony and what you've brought up in me that has been closed from the world. Thinking of you brings a smile to my face and my eyes glaze with happiness. The thought of you, the feeling, the emotion, the bliss...I wish you could feel what I feel, the peace and quiet that sets in my mind and my heart when I think of you. Whenever I couldn't make up my mind suddenly I could see you by my side and right then I knew I'm following my heart, one that which guides me and makes me feel at peace with myself. I wish I could hold your hand, sit right next to you and glare at the beauty of the world. I know a part of you that you don't show the world or anybody. A part of you that has so much love. A part of you which is vulnerable, sensitive. You want to feel it and have someone open it up in you. I wish you do one day and you'll know exactly what it's like to experience this security and love in a relationship with a woman. Being devoted to the One woman who gives you everything. Who brings out the best in you. The love and peace and content that it can give will be so incredible. Your heart will open and

we stop to make photos on the highway. We see herds of the cutest yaks. I try to take a pic of a Tibetan man driving by, but he waves his hands in the air, signaling, "Money, Money!" as I turn my camera away in embarrassment. The Mexican guy in our group, Dario, approaches me, and asks me if I like the scenery. As much as I want to say, *I love it*, I show him my "silence" tag - a habit from the monastery. He looks away, with a silent "Oh, I see".

We make a stop for currency exchange and the Dutch girls try to buy film for their camera. It is so romantic they still have a rolling film camera - because I thought I was the only one still using one. They are hopelessly trying to explain to the Chinese man behind the counter what they want. *In a Kodak store.* I see the problem. We not need words, as we are speaking different languages. I open my camera to show him the film. He is enlightened! ...and gives the girls a new roll of film.

We check into the hotel. Lila and I are staying together. It is clean and nice. I get to shower and wash my hair. I change into white pants and a white shirt. I feel him throughout my entire being. As if his imprint is on me. His hologram.

After eating some Tibetan *momos* - steam dumplings filled with meat and vegetables for Lila and some *then-thuk* - noodles for me, our tour guide picks us up and we walk to the Tashilumpo Monastery. It literally means "all fortune and happiness gathered here" and it is the seat of the Panchen Lama, the second highest ranking tulku (incarnation) lineage in the Gelugpa hierarchy, after the Dalai Lama. A question in my mind arises. If Buddhism does not recognize the existence of soul, why do they recognize the term incarnation and rebirth?....

The monastery sprawls on a hill, with glimmering buildings with rust-color walls and golden roofs. They are the burial chortens of the previous Panchen Lamas. This monastery encompasses a vast set of grounds, with several tombs, chapels and temples. Our guide tells us that later on there will chanting of the monks in the assembly hall and debating in the courtyards.

I ask him whether foreigners can come study here, and he says no...there is no way will the Chinese government allow spies - foreigners to stay.

Our tour guide's name is Tu. I ask him whether he does groups every week. He says yes, he does. He tells me that many Russian tourists go to Kailash Holy Mountain. The road to Western Tibet is very difficult...and sometimes non-existent. It takes a week to get to Darchen by jeeps and the living conditions are poor.

Vajrayana Buddhism found the most favor among the Tibetans - it is also known as Lamaism. It is considered the most complex of all Buddhist traditions. Not only because there are different Buddhas, boddhisattvas and venerated beings, but also because they are worshipped in a variety of different ways. The concept of mystical union with deities which can be achieved by performing mantras, mudras and meditation using a variety of different types of art forms.

I meet Etienne and Sati, the French man, to go eat dinner. We sit in a restaurant nearby, but I am serious about this business - I am only drinking sweet black tea.

We take a walk around town afterwards. I still need to grab hold that I am in Tibet. I have been preparing for this for so long. The energy formed. I guess in spirit I had been waiting for this trip since I was born. And then that powerful energy transformed into meeting another part of my soul - here - now.

And then I follow his calling for me. But why is he not here - now.

Day 4. Gyantze. We are staying at a hotel again, and visiting Palkhor Monastery and Kumbum Chorten - the 100,000 Images Stupa - and according to Buddhist tradition....it has 108 gates, nine storeys and 75 chapels. One tradition identifies the 108 gates with the nine storeys representing space, multiplied by the 12 astrological signs representing time. It looked magical in the pictures. When I see it in reality, it almost looks like a jukebox with memory in it. I feel like this place has underground caves or libraries full of ancient wisdom, way before Vajrayana was even here. The spiritual traditional was Bon - shamanistic and animistic. I feel it could contain sacred knowledge no book in English can carry. Tu tells us that this mystical third-dimensional building was erected upon the order of one of the Gyantze's princes about 500 years ago. Its white tiers built atop one another, laced with golds, reds and blues, grow narrower until culminating in a gold chorten with four pairs of mysterious, piercing blue eyes staring out in the cardinal directions. The eyes look down at me. These eyes.

Palkhor Monastery has a courtyard and contains numerous murals and frescoes - and even a third-dimensional mandala in the chapels and assembly hall. I walk closer to each deity and make subtle connections with them - by ways of holding my fingers in the same mudras. I walk to the statue of Maitreya - white-yellow in color and symbolizing the Buddha's loving kindness and light, he is the future Buddha. The Buddha of Salvation.

Please....please...let James find love.

I bow down my body, speech and mind.
My heart and my spirit. Please help James.

I donate 20 Yuan for a beautiful khata - and a monk blesses my mind. Here, in Tibet. I am happy.

I ask Etienne to take a picture of me standing at the entrance of the Monastery.
I hold my hands in the *Namaskara mudra*.

We return to the hotel.

Sati tells me about his travel plans to Thailand after this trip - he is flying to Bangkok, as is Etienne. He says Thailand is way better than Nepal in terms of Buddhist study. You can show up at any monastery and live, talk to monks, easy and no obligation. He says the center in Thamel is not for real - as you find the true teachers when you GO on a journey to find them, like jungle, or trek...But NOT in Thamel.

He has a point.

This old skinny man is a wanderer. He travels with a bag big enough to fit my running shoes. He eats for 5 Yuan. He tells me that he might even hitchhike back to Kathmandu after the trip. He says Matt and Martina are taking the train to Beijing. I feel I want to travel further. How can I just be putting an end to Asia having only been in Nepal and Tibet?

How can I make this decision. How can I cancel my ticket.

James has not written back. It drives me crazy. I check my e-mail again. It is over.

Before going to sleep, Lila lights a candle and does a ritual. She holds her nose and breathes with the nostril that's open, and then switches them. I tease her into her black magic ritual, to which she laughs. I like how easy and simple she is. She is no-bullshit. I bet if I tell her my story for being here, she would have a lot of breaking down to do.

So we talk about guys. I tell her my view on how women have lost what it is that makes men want them and go after them - their integrity. They feel they owe it just because the guy is being somewhat nice. Women only have one egg per month. We are looking for the right one - to intake the semen and make a baby. Men have plenty. They just want to spread their seed.
-     Gross!
-     So I know. Men take it for granted. They act as if we owe them. But our bodies are sacred. My body is sacred. My body is a temple, which they bow down to. Brace the sacredness of my giving my body to them.
-     Wow.
-     Modern Western girls all go on the pill - dumb and careless. It has all the side-effects: it makes you manly, makes you have your period once in three months, makes you gain weight and stops production of female hormones. It basically makes you think like a man. Whereas the man comes inside you every time.

Lila looks at me in all her attention. - Women just lost the respect for themselves. And they give too much to boys who need a mom. It is all about energy. Women bond so much more during intimacy...and open channels....whereas men are happy to take it and leave.

Tu told me that according to legend, when Avalokiteshvara was looking down from heaven at the world of suffering and weeping at his inability to save all beings from pain, the goddess Tara was born from his tears, or from a lotus floating in one of his tears. In some versions of this legend, two Taras were born from the tears, a peaceful white Tara and a fierce green Tara. The bodhisattva Tara represents all of the miracles of the Buddhas of the past, present and future. As such, these two Taras instilled Avalokiteshvara with the courage to continue his acts of compassion.

Om Tāre Tuttāre Ture Svāhā

Day 5. We will be arriving in Lhasa in the afternoon. We have over 8 hours of driving to do and the highlight is the beautiful Yamdrok Tso – the Turquoise Lake. It is one of the three holiest lakes of Tibet along with Nam-Tso and Lake Manasarovar.

As our jeep makes the kilometers through valleys past cute Tibet-an settlements - small white-washed houses with red roofs and a small part of land where they grow their own crops - the little children run out to wave at us. They are so beautiful. Their amazing round cheeks, with blush = distinct Tibetan.

One of the jeeps was hired by a Swiss family whose daddy works for the Red Cross, they live in South Africa and their kids go to a private Swiss school. Reminds me of my childhood living abroad in the Middle East. We had so much fun before the Gulf War began.

I sit down and glare at the beauty of the lake. It is truly turquoise. Some kids dive in and I would have, as well, had I worn other undies. The Swiss guy is being a weirdo taking a picture of me, thinking I can't see him.

I am trying to get to Tu to ask if he had guided James's group as well. He tells me *Om mani padme hum* means jewel from your heart. *Tug ge che* is thank you. And *kerang de bo inbe?* means how are you? and *na de bon!* means I am well. He tells me that tashi delek - which most people know means hello - literally means "good auspices" whereas the 8 auspicious symbols are *tashi dagye*. As we are sat watching the lake...this week is your access to the future grid...and then you're back into the old frequency. See the future now, while you can. FOCUS, djana. The future. You are in the future. The story has paused last year. You can change it, with the right detail and record.

As we hop back in our jeeps and another four hours of driving we stop for lunch and I ask one of the Macedonian women for a cigarette - as she refuses me, she says she has exactly 10 packs for each day of the trip. She starts looking for a lighter in her purse. I give her my matches and tell her to please have them. I am happy to share matches with her.

Each one of us is a union of all universal energy. Everything that we need in order to be complete is within us right at this very moment. It is simply a matter of being able to recognize it. This is the tantric approach. - Lama Yeshe

...I see the Dalai Lama Palace. So incredible. So changed. It is not the same anymore. We are finally here. After 5 days we finally arrive to the Sacred City.

We settle in the hotel – it is beautiful. I am always thinking of him. We are a nice group but I wish he was here with me. I didn't have to fall in love I could have been friends with him. No I couldn't. Lila and I take a walk down the streets – and find a supermarket it is so funny here nobody speaks a word of English.

-        Look next time I'm just going to start speaking Bulgarian
         'cus I don't care.

We buy some Bacardi breezers to drink later on.

We go to the Internet café and I hope he has written back after so long. Nothing. I check my balance and it seems there's more of an amount blocked than the cost of the ticket. I get furious.

Day 6. I wash my hair. It is almost sunrise. I am excited as we are visiting Drepung Monastery - "Rice Heap". We hop on the bus and I put my headphones on and listen to the few songs I have in my mp3 player. Many Americans felt drawn to Tibet, I've noticed. I did too, as many other Russians, but Americans are a different story. Tibet could be looked at as zero point of our reality. Before you rise, you fall, you hit the bottom, you're in the void. The best Eastern teachers are in the West. This is Tibet. The smell here. The sound. The energy you can almost touch is so powerful combined with the physical changes your body goes through. Not everyone can handle it. I handle it. I am intwine with this energy. I am the exact opposite - I am high, up, in the clouds, I don't need food because my body is so energized with the energy of transcending love.

The power of love.

Tu tells us about Bon - that which emphasizes the purity of space, funerary rituals and meditative practices. Bon has evolved its own parallel literature ranging from exoteric teachings on ethics to highly esoteric teachings on the *Dzogchen* - the Great Perfection.

After we get off the bus, I walk to see the patterns on the rocks from afar – the Mani Stones, rocks with prayers and quotations from the scriptures carved into them. When we walk into the monastery complex, as I spin the wheels with prayers flying out to heaven, I feel how truly and deeply in love I am – I feel how thick my aura had become – I feel its color – bright pink with a hint of peach.

Why do Americans come here. A lot of them. Their past lives, maybe? A population. Could their other aspects be balancing them out, and living their lives here, in this magical and barren land?

In the afternoon we visit Sera Monastery - one of three largest in Tibet, along with Drepung and Ganden it was founded by Lama Tsongkhapa. There is a very special trek, just outside of Lhasa, for 4 days you walk from Ganden to Samye - the very first monastery built in Tibet. A journey from the past to the future and back and forward and back again I will be making in a short while. I can feel it. I can hear it. It is coming.

We will be visiting the highlight - the Potala Palace - the former winter home of His Holiness the Dalai Lama. When he was asked how he feels about being an important spiritual leader, he said he is just a humble monk, living a simple life, and if they want to think of him as the spiritual leader, they can.

We go to line up at the ticket gate for the palace for our visit tomorrow - as we have to bring them our passports. I am very self-conscious when it comes to my passport. It is more about energy. I don't like people touching my personal things. I don't like people looking at my photo. I am attached to it. I argue with the kids in the group to give me my passport back when they start playing around with it. I trade four Swiss passports for mine.

I tell Lila and Etienne I might not be going to the excursion to the main square - the Barkhor Market tomorrow as my stomach aches and I might just relax at home. This place is magical. Perhaps the hotel room can be special too?

I do not want to go to Sera as I feel a stomach ache coming along. I felt it since the morning, actually. I can't make out why. I haven't eaten anything I normally wouldn't. This causes me deep sadness. I feel desperate to write down the things I need to do before this life is finished. As if time is running out.

This journey has to have a different ending.

It has to be everything more than anything I have ever experienced with a human being. And I know...I knew it when I first looked into his eyes...this is going to be a whole different story. Because it is what we will make of it.

But time.

Time is running out.

I feel I need to be somewhere else.

I want to learn to dance salsa, swim with dolphins, skydive, bungy jump, take a Vipassana meditation course, get a PADI card, learn how to cook Chinese food and learn Spanish, before I die. I better hurry up making the plans come true.

No time.

It is up.

Day 7. We are visiting the Jokhang Temple right next to the Barkhor Market - a few blocks away from our hotel and the oldest center and market of Lhasa. I see Tibetans walking around and spinning their prayer wheels. They consist of a closed metal cylinder with a long metal or wooden handle piercing its axis. Tu tells us that inside the cylinder is a text written or printed on paper or animal skin, usually sutras or invocations to deities or sacred charms known as *dharani*. The most popular one is, of course, Om Mani Padme Hum.....with every spin of the prayer wheel = comes one recitation of the mantra. The belief of effectiveness of turning the wheel comes from the Buddhist belief in the power of sound. I see the Tibetans doing full prostrations as their foreheads touch the ground. It is so...powerful...so....touching.

It is...early morning.

Lhasa has indecently earned the name of sinful city....because of all the restaurants, karaoke bars, clubs and casinos. It is contrast to what the true meaning of it is: City of the Deity.

Barkhor Market is a pilgrim circuit - a *kora* - that proceeds clockwise around the periphery of the Jokhang Temple. It is a push and shove of crowds, street performers, turquoise jewelry, jewel-encrusted yak skulls, prayer flags, block prints of holy scriptures, thangkas, Tibetan boots, yak butter and juniper incense all make me feel very very OCD.

The Jokhang Temple is abundant with thangkas and statues. Tibetan art in general, and images in particular, are not meant to serve as accurate representation of portraits, but to express states of the mind and to assist in reaching higher levels of consciousness. Art is intended to represent purity of spirit and to nurture meditation - most images are to guide the meditator in his communication with a particular deity, with the goals of assimilating the deity's attributes and taking the next spiritual step on the path.

I see a statue that beckons my interest - it is the Padmasambhava - it is golden, with mad eyes staring out at you, he wears a blue robe and a red shoulder-scarf. The name literally means "Glorious Lotus Born". Tu says that Padmasambhava's father is the intrinsic awareness, Samantabhadra, and his mother is the ultimate sphere of reality, Samantabhadri . He belongs to the caste of non-duality of the sphere of awareness. His name is the Glorious Lotus Born. He is from the unborn sphere of all phenomena. He consumes concepts of duality as his diet. He acts in the way of the Buddhas of the three times.

Lila stayed at the hotel and didn't come for the excursion. Her stomach aches. She had been feeling strange for a day now, since yesterday afternoon. I asked one of the English girls for an electrolyte-balancing medicine for her. She will be fine before we head to Potala.

-        Okay, your bags in front of you! – says Tu.

We are very conscious of our belongings. We are very *aware*.

The Jokhang Temple is Tibet's holiest shrine. Many thangkas were destroyed during the Cultural Revolution...and were replaced by duplicates.

- I have so many questions I need answers for. Like, why did this happen to Tibet?
- It is the karma of the Tibetan people.

Is that the best they can do? They always say the same thing to tourists. No, I don't expect them to come down with the ultimate truth and wisdom as explanation of the Chinese taking over their land. But it is a conspiracy. It's not meant to be told, or known. Truth is never what we think it is. It the opposite of it.

The Potala Palace was named after Mt. Potalaka - the abode of the deity Avalokiteshvara - the embodiment of compassion - said to be located in South India and literally means "Island Mountain". The Palace stands on Mount Marpori. In front of it stand three big *chortens* - the Buddha, the Miraculous and the Victorious. Other *chortens* house the reliquaries of religious leaders. The Potala Palace contains the most burial chortens of all - those of the past Dalai Lamas. Everything about the chorten has religious significance - in its totality, it embodies the Buddhist concept of true reality, in which the bonds of temporal and physical needs are dissolved. The chorten has a square base, a rounded dome, an oblong slab, a tiered triangular spire, and a small ornament. These elements represent fire, earth, water, air and space.

As we walk in through the frontal stairway, Tu tells us that the Palace took 50 years to build. This specific place was chosen in accordance with the rules of geomancy - and it was the world's highest building before the XX century skyscrapers. The Palace served for the base of the Tibetan theocracy. The outer section is the White Palace as the traditional seat of the government and residence of the Dalai Lamas and the inner Red Palace contains the temples and reliquary tombs of the past Dalai Lamas. It is typical Buddhist architecture. As I stand at the Gate of Great Enlightenment - the entrance to the Red Palace, I feel the powerful need. To be with James. Now.

Inside the palace we pass through rooms where the Dalai Lama studied, slept and ate. There is no access to either room as they are now a museum - and thus they are closed off. But I can see very clearly...golden statues behind glass covers with bills as offering...US dollars, British pounds, Euros, even French francs and even...Russian rubles. My favorite of all are the shelves of Buddhist scriptures. I feel like they are the Akashic records...and a metaphor. Over 200,000 images of the Buddhas and Boddhisattvas adorn the walls of the 1,000 rooms in the former winter home of His Holiness the Dalai Lama.

We leave the palace through the back stairway as I farewell the apogee of this trip.

Most kids in the group are flying back to Kathmandu, whereas me...I am doing it hardcore.

As I restrain from taking a photo with Lila and Etienne I still feel the Nepalese belief that you steal somebody's soul if you take a picture of them is prevalent. I am returning tomorrow and I must get up bright and early.

I find myself sleepless and on the edge of unbalanced emotions, everything I had seen isn't happening, my senses are messed up feeling so much connection and at the same time, feeling so disconnected and unable to pass my message on to him. I am delving and losing myself in all these thoughts and decisions I am making. Should I have not changed my ticket and gone to Thailand instead? Where is he going to be, I don't know. Should I travel to Beijing on a 2-day train like Matt and Martina? How is it that I feel it's me and him, you and I, who are meant to be making this trip together, and making everyone else jealous of our happiness and harmony. Instead these inbred are taking what is mine by right. I am actually so starved right now, I won't sleep unless I get something to eat.

I wander off in the hotel and knock on their door. They are having a party with the Dutch girls and invite me in. Martina is so nice, positive and well-meaning, it is almost annoying. I think that's why Matt likes her, she is natural, impeccable courtesy. I bite on some chips and excuse myself to go to sleep.

Woken up at 5:30 by Lila's watch I say goodbye to her in my mind and walk down the stairs to meet 7 other people also taking the bus. It is going to be a 16-hour trip back to the Nepali border. Get myself together. My love is helping me although I still feel it is gonna be some adventure and it's not over still. There's more to come.

Bus back to Nepal. I should have known better I am making this such a painful experience. All the words linger to me and it is never enough to my tortured heart.

All I can think of is him. I am going back to the minutes with him and remembering his voice, his smile

Our driver is a mad one – given the fact that we took off around 6 in the morning – he is overtaking in the wrong lane, and one of the English girls starts crying and screaming.

- Please don't! Don't go in the wrong lane! - as she gets absolutely hysterical.

I grab her hand to comfort her, as I immediately feel absolutely absorbed into her energy – and I just transferred it and soaked it all in from her. As I break tactile contact I feel overtaken with panic and fear of a road accident.

The driver stops for a pee break – I try to hold it all in, until we stop at a proper toilet – because I don't want the spirits to be angry with me. One of the English girls threw toilet paper after she went – which I am devastated to see.

As we are driving past the view of the Everest – from the point on for another five hours there will be no road – only desert until closer to the Nepali border where jungle begins. I brought no food with me for this one – and the girls have been nice enough to share some bread with peanut butter and bananas – as one finished hers, she threw a banana skin out of the window of the bus.

I keep thinking about his eyes, his voice, his smile, and my heart melts. The iceberg in the place of where his heart is supposed to be, wants to melt under the burning rays of the sun of my love. And I know there was a time that belonged to us. And I feel this connection. It's amazing how quickly after leaving home I met someone who melts my heart. Was it the 4th* day?*

I had been smoking off and on, and keeping the cigarette butts in my bag. I listened to some music on one of the girl's ipods. It seems this journey will never end.

. . .for some reason I just can't think of anything else. And his spirit lives within me. It's in the air I breathe. Taking it all through me.

As we get closer to the border, we see the traffic is stopped. The trucks have been there for a while – there are 7 of them in front of the bus. There is a fallen rock. The builders have bought generators and are trying to break the rock apart to remove it to open the road. We are stuck for 2 hours. A shy Tibetan man approaches the bus and asks me something waving his hands to his mouth. I guess he is asking me for a cigarette. I hand one to him. As he thanks me and smiles at me I can see his dark rotten teeth. The water must be so bad in Tibet. But how? It is home to four major rivers and the water is pure melted snow from the top of the world's highest mountains. The bus finally starts moving and I salute to the workers, with all my gratitude. It feels so easy, from the heart. It feels so good to be grateful. They saved us.

But this journey from Tibet is not over for another 5 hours as we are driving through the jungle to Kodari. The rain starts. The sun goes down. The rain becomes thunder and lightening and the road flooded. The bus gets stuck in the mud as I pray to live and not die here without anyone knowing where I am.

As we are exhausted, hungry, cold and just about unconscious of the bumping of the bus through the jungle, it just hits me how easy everything can be gone. I swear that I wish I never met him – as now I feel all the things so powerfully without being able to share them with him. It makes me so angry that he left me like this – a control issue for him – and a life gone wrong for me.

We get to Kodari and thank the driver as we run to get a bed in the same dormitory we stayed at when we came to Tibet. The girls all have their pot noodle soup and I am starved but too tired to go and get food. Sati and the Macedonian women go to eat and ask me if I wanna come as I say no. I lay in bed smelling all the chicken soup the girls are having and unable able to bear no more, I go to the restaurant next door to find Sati and the Macedonian women eating and order myself some chicken noodles.

I get up in the morning with a funny feeling in my stomach. I get my shit together and meet everyone downstairs to pass immigration. I meet an American couple standing in line at the border with us. The girl says she lives in South Beach. I tell her I gave up Miami to come to Tibet. She asks me where did I travel to, Lhasa? I say yes. She tells me she has travelled all over Tibet. I say "that's hot" as everyone looks at me, puzzled.

We pass immigration as the official collects my permit but does not stamp my passport. NO evidence of being at the Rooftop of the World.

I wonder how they chose who to stamp, and who not to stamp - as everyone in my group got their stamps.

We catch a minibus to the Nepali immigration for 10 Yuan each. We line up at the office as the official tells me I need to pay 5 dollars for applying for a visa without a photo. And so does Sati. The Macedonian woman jumps in to educate me,

-        You knew you had to bring a photo, Djana!

Of course I have a spare photo in my wallet. As did Sati.

We charter a jeep to take us all into Thamel, we will pay 500 rupees each which is a fair price for the distance and the number of people. I don't feel exhausted, tired, and unfortunately sit right next to the Macedonian woman. She gives me a bad vibe, I can feel her astral body of jealousy and envy hitting me with sparse bits of negative emotional energy. She speaks to me in all politeness and brought-on wiseness you would expect from someone her age. She makes me nervous. I give in to the nervousness and start talking about my disappointment of living in the monastery. She taps my back, condescendingly.

-        Don't worry, one day, you will find your teacher.

We make a stop and I have a cigarette of my own. We are only an hour away from Thamel now. I feel bad. The energy is shifting rapidly. And I am the scale of it. If only I had not have booked that ticket to Moscow. I would have all that time to travel. What am I going to do when I return home?

I pray for love. I pray that the Universe gives us a chance. I put all the love and passion I have for this man, into the world, this powerful surge of electromagnetic psychic energy, sending it out to the Guardians.

Please give us a chance

It's what I want more than anything

Please, give my love a chance

There is my hotel!
I shout as I jump out the minibus and say bye to everyone.

I check-in, take a shower and relax. I realize I should perhaps confirm my ticket so I run to the airline office and get a sticker. What a pain to get that ticket, everything is shifting rapidly, my thoughts are all over the place. I ran quickly on the streets of Lalitpur in my blue skirt and flip flops. I feel like a princess in mud. My life...my path is teaching me so much patience.

I catch a rickshaw to take me to Boudhanath as we go past the U.S. Embassy and the Royal Palace. As I enter through the stupa gates, flanked by salesmen and beggars, filthy women with babies asking me to buy milk for their children. The Watchful Eyes again. The massive whitewashed dome decorated with prayer flags dates all the way back to 600 A.D. Its true origin is unknown, and I climb up into its base and stand and look out at the mountains. I see the devout doing their *kora*. Walking around the stupa and praying. In my mind...I can see James.... he carriers incense sticks....and murmurs a prayer.

- Would you mind taking a picture for us? - asks a foreign girl out of the crowd.
- Yes, of course, would you take one for me as well?
- Sure! Where are you from?
- Moscow.
- Oh! We are from Oman!
- Really? One of my best friends is Omani. She keeps telling me to come.
- You should, it is beautiful. What is your name?
- Djana.
- Oh?
- My ancestors were from Saudi Arabia...do you know the meaning of my name?
- No...I don't know...
- It means "heaven".

- Oh! Djannah!
- Yes!
- Do you know the real "djannah" in Oman?
- What is it?
- Salalla.

We take pictures and say goodbyes, perhaps to meet sometime again in our journeys.

Inshalla.

The next morning I go for breakfast to my favorite Weizin Bakery. I see Sati and Etienne.

- Hey! How are you guys!
- Good, come sit down with us!

Etienne is wearing the funniest Hawaiian shirt ever.

- You look so good. So are you flying tomorrow?
- Yes, I am going to Ko Tao to dive.
- Nice shirt!
- Thanks.
- Well we have to get going. So see you around, - says Sati.
- We are all meeting with the Dutch girls tonight. You should come. At 8 p.m. by the Kathmandu Guest House.
- I'd love to.
- See you there.

They leave as I have my morning hot chocolate and croissant.

I walk back to the hotel as a shop with paper-made notepads, photo albums, picture frames and lamps catches my attention. They are "lokta" paper. I wonder why have I not ever seen this place before...I have walked up and down Kantipath numerous times. The salesman invites me to visit the factory. It is a 20-minute ride from Thamel. They make it all by hand. I get a list of wholesale prices.

Day of my flight. Surprise: a strike. I search for a taxi but no-one wants to go for less than a rip-off of a thousand rupees – over seventeen dollars. I get my period and it hurts so bad. I'm running around Thamel searching for a decent price and help for the taxi. I think I'm gonna be trapped in this place forever. A panic runs through me that I might not be able to get over of here.

- Hey, Djana! - a voice in the crowd. – How are you?

It is Luis with the new American guy we had been waiting for. - Hey guys! I wanna stay but I can't I'm in a rush.

I manage to get a cab for 500 rupees and the driver says he will drop me off a five-minute walk from the airport. For the lack of a better choice, I agree. I nervously smoke out of the window. He drops me off in a narrow street.

- Where's the airport? I don't see it!
- That way, walk, five minutes.

I walk on a road closed from traffic, crowded with people making their way to places. I hope this is the road to the airport, but it is nowhere to be seen. A guy on a moped stops by and offers me help. I tell him I have no money to pay him. He says nevermind, he just wants to help. He grabs my luggage and I sit behind him. He drops me off near a bridge, and says I have to walk from there on. I get off, crying and panicking. The pains in my abdomen are driving me crazy.

- Can I help you? Where are you from?
- Russia. I don't need your help.
- I can help you carry your luggage.
- I don't trust anyone.
- Okay, but if you need help, let me know.
- Okay. If you can.
- No problem, - he takes my suitcase and starts pulling it up the road. – Where you flying to?
- Delhi.
- Oh! My sister is arriving from there. I'm going to pick her up.

I line up for check-in. I put 200 rupees in my passport, in case they consider my luggage is over the limit of 20 kilos. The airline rep hands me back my cash and my boarding pass. Apparently the first 10 to check-in can carry more luggage than everyone who checks in after the 10th passenger.

The flight to Delhi is quick and...beautiful. I see the entire Himalayan Range. As the plane lands and the hot air of India in the midst of summer spurts into my face, I wonder if my lay-over of twelve hours signifies that my flight will be on time.

VI. Angels of Love.

Dad meets me at the airport. The local customs search my bags and pick on my brains on what have I been doing IN and how long have I been there. Tell them I was in Kathmandu. They ask me if that's in Nepal. Yes, it's in Nepal. I am now going OUT of the arrivals. Flowers for me are so sweet. Daddy takes me home. I show him the pictures. He likes them. He cooks lunch. I want to speak about James but I shouldn't make him important and bring him into talks as this is going to make everything worse. Better just stay out of him.

- I met a guy.
- Where from?
- New Jersey.
- Why didn't you go traveling together?

I am actually into my idea of bringing and selling the awesome lokta paper lamps in Moscow. I really want to do it. I am focusing on my lamps sales idea.

I think about you at times. I wonder where you are and how your path is unfolding. I remember the feelings I had for you were so incredible and were taking me high. I miss feeling that way. I miss smiling to myself everytime I thought of you or saw you. I missed you even worse when I started the course cus there was nobody I could simply be myself with, nobody I could communicate with as I could with you. There was nobody for real. I miss your ways. I miss my heart quivering when I saw you. I miss your eyes. I miss you.

I want you to feel what I feel. I remember and miss so much of what being close to you brought up in me. I miss you so very much.

Words could not describe the anguish and bitterness I feel now. Part of being alive and a human being, I guess.

I want you to find me and come for me. I wish it had been the time for us. Is there a time to be close to you. Is there a time to look in your eyes, to feel your energy, hold your hand.... It gets me down because it cant happen. Once I gave myself a chance...and it just cant be what I want it to be.

We walk out together and I am wearing a long black Nepali skirt and a black sheer top, covering myself with the white shawl. I am so beautiful. Not because of the clothes. Because of the love that makes me shine. I am so in love. I go to the bank. Feel not so well but calm as I have not slept enough. But it will be over soon. Need a cigarette before I visit the bank.

-    Be careful, sweetheart. You might get yourself dirty.
-    Oh, yes you are right,- as I move away from the wall.
-    It's just that...you're so beautiful in white.

I feel so sensitive and loving. I think everyone around me can feel it. Is everyone psychic these days?!

-    Have a great day!

The charge was indeed made by the airline office rep when they input the credit card number and expiration date in, but will be eventually credited back on the account as no transaction had been made. So one thing off my shoulders. Should I also go to STA and get the refund for the ticket I didn't use? But I will have to get on the subway again and go to the city. I don't feel like it. Maybe another day. I take the subway home.

I wake up the next morning and throw on some dark blue jeans and a white shirt from Nepal with flowers sewn on top. Perfect for this time. I go to STA and get my refund.

I take a walk along Arbat Street – backwards to the Moscow Book House to find a book about Thailand as I am thinking of going there next.

-    Excuse me, is there a map of Italy here? – a foreign man approaches me.

I tell him there isn't one here, but I am going to another book-shop within a 20-minute walk from this one, and he can come with me if he wants to. We walk through the Historic Center of Moscow past the Kremlin and the Red Square to Tverskaya Str. He is from Brazil, visiting his son, a diplomat working for the Brazilian Embassy in Moscow. He invites me for tea in his house. We talk and eat a quick lunch of cold beef and bread. I catch the subway home.

I change. Dad picks me up and we go to the countryside home... it is a wonderful warm sunny summer day. My mom calls me "so ethnic" in my long blue skirt and white top.

...if we are ever past the pain....we will both feel at home at ease with each other. I don't care what form, I just know the feeling. As I always remember. *You.*

Gate, Gate, Paragate, Parasamgate, Bodhi Svaha

...what is happening...I wake up but I don't...I feel I am drowning....in the depths....I feel I am too close to the edge...time is passing in front of my eyes....I see time speed...the clock in the living room is speeding as I open and close my eyes. Life is draining out...something is happening. They call a doctor. I black out....I can't feel a thing.... why is this happening....I'm trying to call you off, make you go away from my mind but I feel you and see you close to me. Please tell me you are okay, please say it is my imagination and paranoia and feeling you is feeling me trying to project my pain is over you, not the truth of it being within me. the energy I feel. I want you to know it. I know I'm drowning again....I'm leaving and floating somewhere....my physical body is giving up...and I'm not scared...not anymore....it is the only place you are at...it is where we always belonged together, as we have, ever since the beginning of creation. Thought, feeling, emotion. Everything sprung out of this. I am not scared to cross over. I see you and I am prepared to go wherever leaving this place means going without returning. I know it will take me elsewhere...it is closer to you. It is with you.

I am prepared to be with you. Dying is the only way to be with you.

Letting go is the only way to be with you.

It is where I belong.

It is where my home is.

My home is where my heart is...

My heart is with you.

-   *Why did he die?*
-   *I don't know. He was not telling us anything. Things were going good for him - he just got a promotion. One day I get a call from his work place telling me hasn't been in for a few days. So I go to his house and open the door and there he is...just laying there.*

...pain taking over me...

-   *...can you not find out what the reason was...*
-   *I did the postmortem examination. And there were no pills, no chemicals, no alcohol in his blood.*

I burst out in tears.

-   *But how...and why...*
-   *Ildar had told me Chingiz has been having heart murmurs - hums - he said his heart beats as normal but suddenly it stops for a few seconds and then goes on again.*
-   *How...could he...*
-   *...we have always helped them you know and how could he keep something like this from me...??*
-   *He never told...??*

As the car pulls into the driveway I remember I forgot to buy flowers.

-   *Ildar says he didn't want us to worry. But I am a heart surgeon. And I couldn't help my own son???*

-     *What about Elmira?*
-     *She turned out to be a very selfish one. She never called us since he died. She hasn't asked if we had been okay. She only cared about herself. I mean, if Chingiz had been coming home and he knew there was somebody there who cared about him - not to mention - love him - it would have never happened.*
-     *They were not living together?*
-     *No, from what I know the first New Year they spent apart and the second New Years Elmira took off in his car. She didn't want to stay home. She wanted to be out there partying. She didn't take care of her husband or the house. She wasn't a homey girl. Did you know that Chingiz brought laundry for us to do?*

I get out the car and walk to the grave. The old man bursts out in tears. It hurts to see him like this. I can't believe it. How much he loved his son. And they have been through so much together. And now he is gone. And nothing can bring him back.

Are you feeling better?

...as I open my eyes and sit up. I find five missed calls from the Brazilian man.

I had been away. But much linear time had passed?...

...when time is running out...and the last moment you have to tell that person what they mean to you and how special they are and how they made you feel. James. James.

Part II. I was thinking to myself, how is it that I meet someone I felt so much at first sight and felt deeply connected to, experiencing a psychic jolt and my soul rising again from the ashes of pain and sorrow. I felt so comfortable being next to you, I haven't experienced this in this lifetime with anyone.

I had left the course behind, taken the trip to Tibet, loving every minute of it. Many thoughts have come to mind about you, I wondered if you saw the same things I have and gone to the same places. I love your pictures :)

I spent a few days just being by myself, listening to music, writing and drawing. Your spirit was right next to me all the while and it felt so good and comforting. I just wanted to be with you. You were the first thing I thought of when I woke up and the last thing before I fell asleep. Just holding the image of you next to me. My heart still beats fast when I think of you, and I know there's nowhere I wannabe but with you, wherever you are. At times I feel I am slowly letting go of my feelings for you, because it's hard to focus on other things as I just want to feel the peace and quiet that has set in my heart and soul ever since I looked in your eyes, but what if the world came to an end tonight...I'd know where I'd want to be... with you. And there are no words to describe how bad it feels because you don't see me the way I see you. It's just so rare that such a thing is mutual, but when it is....Oh! Nothing can come between the two. Because we are One. :)

I hope I can still keep my heart open; afterall, I'm in this alone, but even though I feel bitter, you were worth it. You are worth so much more and you deserve someone special who's gonna love you unconditionally and truly, with all their heart and soul, give you everything you need to feel complete, make your beautiful wife and bear your children.

I truly care about you, nothing is ever going to change what having met you has brought up in me. It was just so incredible, I am so grateful to the person who has guided you to to the monastery. It was meant to be for me to experience what I have. I am so happy.

For the times we never had, or had but forgotten, It's all going now....and as much as I want you for myself....all of you, heart and soul, body and mind...memories are coming back to me slowly as my mind clears a little bit....But it's my heart that matters, the one that guides me. Wasn't it what you said once...:D embrace what I am giving you, please don't hold back, don't reject what I'm sending you with this letter. Don't feel bad. Simply take it. Open your heart and take it. There's no time to hesitate, no time to hold back. See how it feels...It's meant to make you feel good. Thats what I want for you, to be happy and content, peaceful and calm. You are so fortunate. You are so wonderful just as you are. You are so beautiful. The world is at your feet, you just have to take it.

As if I looked into your eyes for one moment...A glimpse into your soul...That has taken me high...
Thank you, James"

III. I have a message for you from your Angels....They're saying you are going through and evaluation and deep delving desire to understand the way things truly are. They're saying you're not content nor happy with everything you have, it just gives you no pleasure; and you get mad at yourself for not being happy with what you have, your logic is constantly monitoring your experience, filtering what is good and what is bad for you, from its own perspective. Thinking two steps ahead.
You can always either construct, or destroy. (No pun intended! Honest!) I know how you feel, because I have processed it and taken it through myself involuntarily at the monastery. I don't quite see why it has happened and how it connected to me, but my job is to tell you what I know.

Your process is that of closing yourself and not letting people see who you truly are. Even though you have many friends, it's the mask you put on when you are around them. Nobody ever gets to see who you
really are. It's a wall that you put around yourself, many years ago. Somehow it seems to me it was before you were about four years old. You don't get to see this wall, it expresses itself in form of not being able to give from the heart, trustfully and openly, but doing it as more of an obligation, based on guilt.
You're closed, unavailable, unable to give the smallest piece of your heart to a woman. You're into yourself. You want to be by yourself,

free of attachment. You don't trust women. Is there a part of you very selfish and arrogant? There must be.

I feel that having the good looks of yours is a burden at times, because it's so easy to get the affection of the opposite sex. And it seems to me you take it all for granted. Somehow there's nothing new to you, everything is all over and boring. Nobody has ever taken the time to know you for real, and you would never even give them that chance. I saw it in your eyes for one split second one night in New Orleans -- I denied it at first, but my mind is slowly clearing from the clouds of infatuation with you --and I see it now. I know what it feels like as well. It's almost like you have to live your life with things coming to you, and in the years you get used to them, you don't have to work hard to get it. Its great, isn't it? There is nothing wrong with this, but you feel you want more, don't you? I felt this was the reason you dropped what was going on at home, and flew all the way across the Atlantic to have a simpler day after day, with true human values. I know how you feel...I really do. It's the part of you that can only open up and come out when your dad is not around... When you don't feel him watching you, judging you, controlling you.... But James, even when he isn't, he still is. He is within you. He is you. I have gone through so much with my controlling, codependent dad, from hating his ridiculous ways of expressing his love in shouting instead of holding me, when he wanted to, but couldn't. We haven't really been nurtured to express our feelings openly. And it breaks my heart!! So many people are struggling with their parents still affecting them when they have kids of their own. Its so messed up! Truth is, nobody knows what goes on behind closed doors.

I know you're suffering, in your heart, it feels wrong. You don't have to shut people off and remain lonely, covering up for that big part of you yearning for love with a mask of humour and openness. Find that part of you that saves love and give it to the world. Let it come shining. Give the gift of you to the world.

I know you can do it, if you really want to. Oh James. I'll always be there for you if you ever feel you need me. Something connected to my soul so deeply, it's not easy to understand why its happening to me, or let it go.

I'll keep writing to you when I have to. I have to."

-   How are you?
-   In love.
-   Who is it?
-   The guy I met in Nepal.
-   I thought it wasn't anything.
-   It is everything. I connect to him. His spirit is with me all the time. I start typing when I think of him...
-   ...you start typing when he comes to you mind?
-   Yes...it pours out...
-   It's very interesting...I have been reading a book....a therapist...he reads past lives and karmic lessons. He says that after a consultation he starts writing. He channels messages when he types...unconsciously...
-   ...
-   ...he says that the feeling of love is very important....does your ability have to do with the feeling of love?
-   Oh My God....yes!!...
-   ...he says that it is the feeling of love that gives us the ability to really deeply understand and help heal others. If you love someone or someone loves you, then things come your way, everything goes well as long as you give in to the love. But if you fight, reject or kill it, it hits back.

Dad is laying on his bed with his arm up. I notice a dark ball on his underarm.

-   What is that?
-   Where?
-   On your underarm!

It's a tick. He must have gotten it from the trekking he did in the countryside the other day.

- We need to see a doctor!
- Come, let's go. Can you hold me?

We catch a cab to the hospital. I panic wearing my father's coat, stumbling through the streets after a summer rain. A tick can make you a physically and mentally disabled vegetable. Talk about being what you eat. It scares me to be here. He was here a few months back when I had premonitions. I traveled to the States right after. I had to. I was so scared. As we sit in the waiting room I...pray...I think of my ancestors. My grandfather. Dad is being examined. Ticks around Moscow are not encephalitis. Slowly lubricating the body of the bug and gently removing him from the skin. *Thank you, my Angels.*

I feel such reverence. My father. I touched the future and the past when I had seen a tragedy a year earlier. And now he is here. And I am with him. I am with him._Once I touch possibility it saves us as our bond and my loyalty for him is such a transforming multi-dimensional experience. Nothing else comes close. And I love James so very...very much....that I feel his pain....but he does not love me....and he does not recognize our connection......

- You saved me, Djani.

As we return home I open my inbox.

Re: Part II. I am a kind of lost for words right now. I have read the previous e-mail a few times and I have read the most recent one just before.

I am close to tears. And I am not saying this for you to feel bad. Far from it. Just to let you know that you HAVE touched me.

There is obviously something very special about you.

You are gifted to great extent. Do you know this?

Reading and 'listening' to what you are saying makes me just want to feel the same.

But there are issues which you have somehow adeptly recognized.

I think you have noted them in the last e-mail so I am going to go to it as I want to address them.

IV. The Angels are saying that I was meant to channel to you what I have, for being me given that ability must be of use for you. You were in my life to help my finally realize the gift which I have struggled with for many years as it was not the time for me to be conscious of it. They are also saying, that because you are not in a point in your life to embrace our connection as your experience is different from mine, and basically your logic will not accept it, we were not meant to be. I was placed in your life at a difficult time when you are focused on working out your issues; there is really no place for me in your life. Because of that, you cannot embrace it or feel the same, and thus missing a soulmate. It was predetermined, that was the general idea behind our meeting. It's happened exactly as the Universe made it to happen. Will not meet anyone like this again, as the energy one creates by not taking what is coming to one but is not meant to be resonates in the imprint of memory to create the future based on past actions.

The turn of Saturn has brought us together, but it really never did.

forgive me for telling you this. I have to let you know what I know. For the first time, I really feel I can. I realize I cant be yours, and you cant be mine. I know in a different life we could have made the world for each other. I was walking in the streets of my hometown and nothing existed for me, I just felt like my life is with you. My life could have been loving you, understanding you, feeling that having you next to me makes me feel complete and there's just the two of us. Well, one. :).

There's nothing I want, need and wish for more than a wonderful man like you to love and care for...I really felt there's a big part of you that needs someone who can give, and from the right person, you can take, it would just come naturally. And it has opened my heart to you. With you I felt for the first time my mind isn't controlling me, not screaming at me to wake up and stop living in the illusion that I could love someone. It felt so true. For the first time, I saw someone I felt I could make a life with. But it's not my path. It's not our path. Its not our destiny. There's no we, there's no our. It hurts so bad. But...what else is new. It's not meant to be. I have to brace the logic understanding and give it up. But it really isn't true. I will never really give up on you. I cant. I know what I felt. The image of you in my mind telling me I had set myself up to break my heart. Such a silly little girl. I'm going through all these emotions and all I can do is let it all out in my drawing. Geez I never had this before. They actually turn out pretty nice, it's like a whole gallery of my wondrous mind. Lol. All my energy centers run wild when Im talking to you. I been smoking like a chimney lately!! Somehow the thought of you always makes me feel so good, always puts a smile to my face, I want to run to you and see your smile, hear your laughter and feel your loving embrace. Look in your beautiful eyes and fall in love with you every time like the first time. Want you to carry me in your arms, feel so close to you. Be the One for you.

Damn I cant become one of these women so miserable covering their misery and emptiness becoming freaking bitchy ice-cold heartbreakers; and piling themselves with work and career; all because their true purpose of being a loving wife and mother is not happening. Oh geez. I wasn't made for that. But hell knows now. It's messed up. I feel nothing is worth anything. If my life has to be without loving every day, every minute, I'd rather not live at all. Actually I still wonder how I made it to this day. There's no point in living if you can't love, and be loved. Its...all or nothing

Damn I feel like I'm meant to wander around all my life without love. How can one keep an open heart when all they know is pain? Shutting down is the only way to keep safe. (Ego talk) Daah. Not meant to love, give, be loved back, make a life with a man I love. I have learnt so much from so much pain, I have learnt to accept and deal with, I managed to open that part of me that has so much love to give, only to find that there is no-one to give it to. So what was the point then?!

What was the point of making this tremendous, exhausting journey? I'm so drained of coping, dealing with, being strong. I just want to be in touch with my true inner self. How is it that I feel so comfortable to tell you things I never told anyone. I know you'd never do anything to deliberately hurt me or betray my trust. I just know it. I know I can trust you my deepest feelings.

I once had some sort of premonitions, a tragedy, but I couldn't make it out. I saw some bits and parts and time and place. Then it happened, and I wasn't there...and it broke my heart into tiny pieces cus I was powerless to change it, it was not for me to decide a destiny, when I tried, but couldn't warn them before its too late. It still breaks my heart to this day and I feel so weak. I will never face this pain again. Ever. Oh there it goes, closing down my heart. Actually I feel this pain everyday, it never really goes away. It's just that somehow I had been tricked into thinking that love can heal that pain, and its made me want to go on, cus I realized how precious life is. How precious is everything we have, but never really know or appreciate till they're gone. Thats when I knew I will never ever take anyone or anything for granted, I wont have to lose it to know what I have. Once I faced the edge. It became so clear as to how ridiculous it was to waste myself on dysfunctional people, situations, whatever my mind could focus on to keep me from what is truly important, searching for answer as to why; which gets you nowhere, and realized overnight what I truly should do with my life. Cus we have truly been given so much beauty, talent, gifts, health, family, people who love and care for us; but alotta times we don't know it. And thus cant take... gratefully.

My Angels I knew that are no longer with me, who have helped me grow, still feel them watching over me and guiding me, helping me get through the worst, and helping me brace the universal truth. But at times I think I'm trying so hard to brace something I will never really accept, because I can't tell them how much they mean to me, as they are ephemeral spirits in my imagination and what we had has vanished into the void. Just taken away, in a snap of a finger. And all for what?

I just took a break from writing....My mind just calmed down, you know why? Cus I was thinking of you. I always do. And I'm smiling again :)) One more thing I'd like to tell you. I was so determined to be by myself, and have been for looong. And was happy, everyday just getting better and I felt so happy to just be with me. Free, detached, noone to worry about, noone to give me sh*t, wanting some from me, etc. I was going to take that course to finalize a brace of a philosophy to live by. Yes I was prepared to go into a monastery, lol. But how was I to know I was all but setting myself up to meet you (or it was a ploy of the Universe to mess up my mind --depends how I look at it LMFAO!!!), who's triggered thoughts and feelings I've kept deep inside, and no guy has made them come out the way you did, and for the first time my mind had no power over my heart -- it felt great to give in. Cus you're wonderful, and it makes me wonderful to be in love with someone like you. Makes me laugh of joy, I swear :--))))))))) Oh sweety, I'm just a girl in love. And it's wonderful. If only I could be inspired like I am, everyday, till the rest of my life."

I feel high as my entire body is invigorated with the feeling of transcending love. I don't want to eat as my body is feeding on the most nourishing element in the Universe: love. My soul sings on a high harmonic as I flip through his photos on myspace, they are so beautiful, they are new, he must have just posted them. The wild, free spirit inside the body of a beautiful man, the searcher for the Ultimate, looking hot in his trekking gear listening to music on his ipod. I love his three-day stubble, his long curly hair, a hologram of his beautiful face in my hands, subtly kiss his lips, he closes his eyes, gives in to me; the journey from Ganden to Samye and back, chopsticks and pandas. The sun setting down the Himalayas, Zhomolungma and Nam-Tso Lake. Yak at Drak Yerpa cave. Prayer flags. The power of the images hitting me like the sound of a gong and resonating from deep within...

and I love him with every fiber of my being.

V. Ok, I know I'm getting on your nerves now. Don't mean to. Just miss you and feel like writing to you.

I'm all passed the emotions, now thinking quite radically. I think you're a great guy, as well as a very strong personality, you're just what any girl would want, and any girl would be so lucky to have you. I think its great that you're so determined to be by yourself, know you grow the most when you are. Have I told you I think you're great?

Also when I first saw you, apart from the incredibly strong deja vu, familiarity and closeness that hit me, as if I had known you all my life, I also 'saw' a woman standing by you. At first I was convinced someone was there with you, but then obviously I knew you was by yourself. From back then<<can you tell me whether there was/is a girlfriend at home? Or someone on your mind from the past/present? Let me know if it is either of two. I'll tell you why I'm asking. I need to understand why I 'saw' her. Sorry if its confusing, it's not less confusing for me, than for you. Hope you can help me...Thanks xx

Re: V. You should know that you are not getting on my nerves. Your e-mails feel to me as though they are a blessing.

I believe you are very special but I don't know why I am a person who influenced you. Although it seems in a way I helped you. If so - then I am happy.

Before I forget: the images you send are amazing. I would purchase them and hang them up.

You are very intelligent and articulate. I think you speak better English than me. I'm serious.

I have to say this is a curious time for me to be asked about other girls. Back at the monastery there was no girl. I broke up with a wonderful girl before I had left home, I didn't love her, I was not thinking about her.

But right now I am facing quite a difficult decision as I am supposed to meet a girl from NY (met on-line) in Thailand at the end of August. However, there is another girl that I would like to meet in SE Asia as well.

I can't figure out what I should do and this has become a problem for me as I have developed strong ties with each girl. I always try and follow my heart and do the right thing - but I find myself clouded in this predicament. And in this case I don't know perhaps I must change my travel plans to go to Thailand to meet this girl b/c I just want to follow whatever path lays ahead of me. I am also scared to meet one girl if that means not meeting the other b/c you never know what can happen. Obviously I can always go back to NY to meet the girl I am supposed to meet in Thailand one day (this is not guaranteed though). I have already committed to meeting the NY girl in Thailand. She will be there regardless of me being there, and thinks I will meet her for a week now. I have told the other girl about the NY girl and she is very cool with my honesty but of course does not want me to make plans with her till I know what I am doing.

I am perplexed. I understand there are way worse situations and I don't know if a wrong answer exists in this situation however I had fallen physically ill these past few days and I believe having to make this decision is part of the reason.

This is all happening as I am getting these insightful e-mails from you. And I wonder if I should tell you or not (due to the vagueness of the circumstance). I hope it doesn't upset you that I told you about other girls. You asked me so I told you. You also may be the only one to help me but it is a decision I obviously must make myself. I am also scared of the walls against love which you have so accurately stated. I hope that I can open up if it is right with one of these girls.

I read your e-mails hoping that they can shed some light on where I am at right now, as I am confused (as you say), and trying to figure things out. I actually printed your e-mails as I needed to read them in private.

I truly feel like you are self-actualizing before my very own eyes - and yours. You are coming to peace with yourself and your powerful gift.

As it also seems to me that you are working things out at a rate I can only dream of. But you also scare me. Saying that there is no place for you in this world? Do you really believe that or are you working it through as well.

Perhaps someone with your gifts might have a harder time finding their place, but think the opposite - w/o you in the world, would seem to be a big mistake.

I hope I helped with your question about the girl w/o giving out irrelevant information. I am curious to know what you think.

Thank you for you persistence in writing to me. I will say it again that you are not getting on my nerves. YOU should know this and know this well.

so thanks to you.

With all my love and best wishes that I can possibly send to you at this point in time.

"Write to him. Now"

VI. The underlying reason for your ongoing analysis about your significant others' behavior towards you lies deep within a process named pride. You can be eating yourself with someone's words, or a look they gave you, anything that can trigger the mechanism directed to destroy your true beautiful self, and let your ego take over. Why did they do that, why did they say that that, etc.,etc., just endlessly going and going going and never stopping. It is very exhausting. You do, though, understand that they didn't mean it, however the ego presses on.

If you introspect for a minute....can you remember you started opening up a bit when I was close by? Apart from my empathic ability which has finally come to my consciousness because of and thanks to you, I realized I may have been experiencing YOUR process within myself. Geez. This is so interesting. Well where is me then? Am I a part of you? Or are you a part of me? Are we parts of each other? Or am I a mental patient, lol. That would make it a lot easier if I were :D

Look, I know giving you so much information all at once might be hard on you, but the reason I am is because you're ready to hear it and learn from it, what you can/want, or you can always reject it and throw it out. Just know that I'm in the process of discovering a lot of new things about my self right now, and I really do need your thoughts, if any. Please."

I press send and see a new e-mail from him received five minutes ago.

Re: VI. You are right. I am ready to hear all of this. It's why I can't believe it that I am receiving these e-mails from you. I never expected it.

Where did you come from? Seriously, are you an angel?

It seems that we are both helping each other. I don't know why or where it is leading to but it is so beautiful.

I do remember opening up to you. I would not just tell anybody personal stuff. But I felt alright telling you.

And yes, I suppose it is pride. I always just looked at it as being way too self-conscious. I overanalyze situations until I am sick. I drive myself crazy as to why people look at me a certain way and I am too sensitive to what other people are thinking. I am not sure if this is a gift yet yet I have been told it is. You have realized your abilities finally - and in a good light.

This is a lot of info. but it is great. Again, where did you come from. I can't understand. I feel blessed to have met a person whom I think is enlightened to some extent.

I guess I don't feel like I deserve help and or attention. I feel I am still at the same place I was when I left home.

Yet, I am of course so happy to receive these e-mails.

I hope I am replying well enough. I am a bit overwhelmed, but would not want to read any less from you."

VII. There's a very powerful connection between us that transcends time and space. We are given a chance right now by the Universe to take it and make something out of it or let it run its own course. What do you want out of a relationship? Are you just searching for yourself with meaningless acquaintances and endless romances? I know what I want. I want you. I want what you brought up in me - the right thing for me. I know I can go with you to world's end, I can stand with you through anything. Because our bond is beyond our logic understanding, we can touch it only if we let our subconscious memories come out. Oh no I'm getting the vomit syndrome. It's so powerful it makes me wanna puke. I think my pressure is jumping up and down, as connecting with the unconscious is hard work when you're just starting out. I know I want someone when I look into their eyes I know they're the One there is for me, the Only and only man. It can never be too much than I can take. I'm ready. I saw a part of my soul spark in you, a part of me born on a separate continent but still maintaining a deep connection, as we are experiencing multidimensionally, and where I am, there you are; a soul in a group, having the same experience. We are all searching. And I have just found you. And you've given so much by being there. I want to tell you this everyday...in your eyes I found a beautiful reflection of myself.

James, if only you could understand what I feel. I dream about you every night, the only time I rest, cus when I wake up it starts all over again - seeing you in front of me, feeling this incredibly strong pull towards you and a connection that is beyond our normal understanding. If only you felt this tiny bit of what I felt when I first saw you. It gets me down every time cus I have to keep reminding myself this is not mutual, when in my heart I feel you can hear me. There IS a part of you that does feel this connection too. It is that part of you which you put down many years ago, and it's suffocating inside you in the prison of your logic. It is that part of you which connected to me as it wants you to know it's there --in a human form. It is that part of you that keeps telling me to keep writing to you, to bring it to your logic. Better yet, awaken your intuitive part to take over your logic.

This can only happen once in a lifetime, that you find someone "in-passing" - the one person thats there to guard and watch over you, understand you as if you have been together for lifetimes. And we have, I knew it the second I saw you, and when you came to say goodbye, I couldn't hold it, I told you straight. I know I struck you, but there was no other way. The connection is wherever you are, you feel that person, because your bond transcends 3D reality; all you do is think of them, and they are there by your side. Cus thats what I feel - you - your thoughts, your feelings. It's alotta emotional work, at times its hard to distinguish where I am, where is my imagination and where you are. I am learning to read accurately now. It's so much mental work. But my deep love for you gives me strength and will to get through this mental torture. This love is so much more than an emotion, it's everything for me. It is knowing you, seeing through you as you are part of me, as we have shared this deep understanding and connection, so close and sacred. It's only mine and yours. That part of you that speaks to me...right now

All I can do is channel what I know to you. It is such hard work, that's why I said there's no place for me in this world as my job is something else. Oh James. It is so powerful, I don't know if I can take this. I can't concentrate on my life, all there is is you.

Nothing else.

Do you understand what I have for you?

A true gift from the Universe, and I have never been more ready than I am. I just wish you had been too.

You'll get better just as you make up your mind, just as whatever the Universe is trying to tell you sets in your soul, and remember to listen to your heart. Once your heart beats in the direction of someone or something, thats the road to take. Be very honest with yourself. And let you logic come down for a second, so your heart can lead you. And these are way more than words. Have you ever tried giving up control and planning? It's an interesting way to see where it can take you.

As for the girl I saw, she had brown hair I think, medium-height. Anyone we know? Let me know.

VIII. Feel like I'm gonna drive myself completely crazy with this. I hope you don't worry though, I've been through much worse. What I'm going thru right now is beautiful. It's the high and energy soar I felt when I stood close to you. I just want to feel it again, cus my soul rose so high in frequency, opening up my senses, we must have both felt it. I just did some more research, and found its what happened when our grids connected. You felt something hitting you? I think it was stronger for me, and it has made me so much more psychic. Oh God. See this is what I'm talking about, you're helping me be more psychic and clairvoyant. Ahh!! You're the gift of the Higher Powers. How did this happen?! You should know what you mean to me by now. And its my secret...will you keep it?

I can't help it. Why does a sweet, kind-hearted guy with a truly genuine soul like you have to wander around the world, seeking for answers? This is my question to the Universe. I am sick and tired of this. Do you have any idea what kinda like really messed up guys there are out there!? Sure you do, you're from Jersey :P JUST KIDDING. And they're not worth the dirt off your shoes. If that makes sense, pardon my French. Tell me the truth, you have loved, haven't you? When you were about my age? I feel it. I see it in your eyes in the picture with the elephant. She's there. Or am I just crazy? I need to understand.

Hope to get some sleep tonight. See you in my dreams...

IX. I never shut my eyes for one minute last night. I was thinking of you all the time. How are you feeling? Are you feeling any better?

I can't type anymore/I feel you in my mind/Think we are talking right now.

I can't say anymore than I have. I feel I've said all the important things. I've recognized a soul connection with you, I can't even describe what I feel every time I remember looking in your eyes. James....I can't describe what I felt just a while ago. I'm asking myself how didn't I see it before.

...did you go through a lot of emotional pain when you were a teen? Did it seem to have no cause, as all the things in your life had been settled as you come from a good genetic background and a well-off family, and you felt you was in it by yourself, for many years you remained unheard?

Think it's known as clinical depression in America. Chemical imbalance in the brain? I looked at your picture last night....and it hit me...There's so much pain in your eyes. I'm an idiot for not seeing this before. Surprisingly it's my favorite shot of you - the Buddha eyes. Did you also have very good strong health when you were a baby, boy, teen, adult and then you developed an illness out of the blue?

You know what I felt when we was at the monastery? That for some reason you did not belong in Jersey. Are you sure you from there? I know how this question sounds. When I first saw you, I was struggling

thru the information that kept coming cus I was getting lost as I did not get a sense of Earthy location from you. You were from somewhere else. Didn't you feel for a long time you did not belong in this world?

As if your home is elsewhere?

I can make out pretty clear that you must have been given a lot of shit about your emotional problems by counselors. Simply because...I have. I think if you went through what I went through, you must be a very strong human being to go through with it and still be here today. I think you have powerful Guardians over you. Just schh...I never told you this. Sometimes they want to remain unknown, quietly doing their job watching over you. But you'll feel them. They have not opened themselves to you, as you have been out of touch with the metaphysical side of reality, but you are really starting to open to it. I am another aspect of your soul, and a mirror to show you YOUR empath ability -- which has been put down as your ego took over to defend itself and made this 'oversensitivity' to other people, which is another manifestation of pride; but it really is your ego messing up the creative, intuitive part of your personality. You have the genuine gift of empathy, but you haven't been given someone that you have been for me - the one who truly opened it up, brought it to my consciousness.

Allow the Universe to lead you. Your soul does connect to mine, as do our energy grids. It is your soul that is trying to break free from your mind prison. It is strong, I feel it touching me like a magnet, right now, where you are I don't know, but I feel you

It is your depression that keeps you from truly bonding with a woman. You sabotage with the right girl...because you're depressed. I think you need to be by yourself for a while, you really don't need anybody, except the soulmate you are searching for, the one who can open your heart. This is your only true need regarding girls at this point.

Because you're depressed, you cant see the true wonderful guy inside you. Your ego takes over and says, "I'm a great guy, I have alotta fun, I'm open, I have many friends, I date, enjoy women, my life is great, I've achieved alot". Your pride, which manifests in eating yourself and feeling not worthy of, also arrogance, feeling worthy of way more but that which does not exist or no-one can give you, is not really

you, it's your ego. You're changing girls that are wrong for you cus you don't feel you deserve any more than you are getting, or you are picky cus neither is good enough for you. It's all the same story, just

different plays. Neither of them has ever touched your heart. It is like your defenses.

Some people, who you have a soul connection with, can see your true soul. They are like your metaphysical helpers on your journey. This is what I see. Your beautiful, shining soul. It hurts me you have experienced pain and sorrow, and there was nobody to help you through.

Souls like us are all over the world - and we are suffering teenagers, in need of so much understanding and love.

I came from the same soul group, or source, as you have. I am here to help you through as you are lost and you need help. This is such an important journey for you, and you really are opening to alot of new information.

I can't say it enough to you. There's an incredible part of you that you're putting down. Someone has to make it come out. Cus you were a little angel when you were first born. Still are, just need to grow your wings back.

VII. Twin Souls

My taxi is waiting. It is raining. The dishes are unwashed. The decision made, the path chosen.

I have no cash to get a coffee and smoking is prohibited. Only that. He is with me all the time. I am strangely hoping to force a change that is inevitable shoot-down of his energy around me. We are meant to be together in the United States, where we both belong together – not apart. We are meant to travel and live our lives as One – always. Loving him makes me fulfill my genetic encoding and program in this grid = finishing to evolve and ending this experiment. Loving him opens up my gifts as this is how the Universe sees us grow. I am smiling to myself as Universes are coming together in wormholes = sparks come together and recognize one another from other dimensions. As our root grid is overloaded with materialism, and the higher grid of the seven grids is the higher realm, depending on the level of development and awareness of a person can one recognize such connection. I believe we are connected through the heart which has opened = taken me beyond physical reality. His connection to me had been through the Y = yellow center of emotions. When we held hands thoughts and emotions came intwine, parallel worlds and dramas paused to watch us rise above all that has been. The energy was zooming in and out, it was zinging in my ears as I felt us rise in frequency up on a harmonic. The sound was Z.

Back on Earth. The plane has landed. It is so hot and humid. Nauseous. Rare memories come into mind. I arrive to an empty dark apartment, finding the light switch after an hour of searching around the place. The landline isn't working. My old sim card is out of service. I'm about to start panicking. I so haven't prepared. Thankfully and surprisingly there's some peanut butter and chocolate spread in the cupboard. A cup of sweet black tea will make things right. So thirsty.

...a wave comes over me and hits me...all over...This is the realest fit of pain, I am trying to get a grip on myself to stop this melodramatic mood but I don't have my computer I can't type I don't have my journal I don't have pens and I'm

> *hurting so much*
> *You're not letting me love, I feel that part of me dying inside*
> *Because you're part of me*
>
> *You're a wonderful soul, and you need someone to help you heal. I'm here.*
>
> *Your soul speaks to me, keeps me from sleep.*

...we know so little of reality.

If you had to pin-point the pain you felt last night...could you? Could you say, this is the thought and memory that is hurting my aching heart and drained spirit. We had been so close already, there's no way we can get any closer, no point in being close as we don't grow. So much better to stay apart and suffer – oh gee! We learn from pain. Pride and urge to analyze block psychological understanding of this. But we are truly so close and possess the urge to compound facts and knowledge into breaking down this experience into pieces and synthesizing this as we are parts of one mind, or soul. And nothing comes close to what we have, and it perseveres.

The Celestine Prophecy consists of Nine Insights.

The First Insight stipulates that by synchronicity people are led to realization and opening up to the spiritual unfolding side of life. The Second Insight says that the world is about to change. Where Intention

Goes, Energy Flows. The Third Insight says that we experience not a material, but a dynamic energy in the Universe. The Fourth Insight says that many times people cut themselves off from taking energy from the greater source and feel weak and insecure. To gain energy they manipulate others and as we successfully dominate others in this way, we feel more powerful but they are left weakened and often fight back. This is competition for human energy and is the cause of all conflict between people. We will stop building ourselves up by taking energy from others. There is another source - inside. But we have to really connect with it. "Open up". If you open up enough, it changes the way you see the world. But you have to really believe this experience exists. Open yourself to the possibility that there is something more, right here, in front of your eyes. The Fifth Insight says that the right person will come along, there is always help out there. You have to stay alert. Expect it. Be amazed and feel and see the beauty of everything around you. Thus you are connecting to that higher source of energy. The Sixth Insight says that we are part of a larger flow of evolution. We are here to do something. If we are true to that purpose, we'll help move humanity towards a better world. The Seventh Insight - we are given guidance to know our destiny: intuition, dreams, signs to follow our paths to that destiny. The Eighth Insight is that when two people meet and a relationship begins there is competition if one becomes insecure and starts to become controlling. And so instead of taking energy from each other - you give it. All the time, no matter what. You feel the energy moving to them.

I had grabbed the torch of the connection and gone the way I was told to. Now trying to psyche and foretell the future and minimize the X factor :o)

It is one thing to just give energy, but if we give it to somebody who is also giving it back, then we build energy among ourselves. It amplifies, back and forth. If we were all doing this, humanity will take another step in evolution. That is the Ninth Insight.

VIII. The Twist of Destiny

All things are like a river. We never enter the same river twice.

X. I had been taken away from the opportunity to write to you for a while. It seems the Universe is monitoring my every step. How is everything? I hope you're doing well it's just that sometimes it feels to me something's procrastinating you. Dunno.

Hey I loved reading the Celestine Prophecy while frying in the summer sun in the Mediterranean. Every time there was a line I thought was so interesting I underlined it and put the book down to embrace and feel the incredibility of having had that experience with you.

I did write a few passages....when I had one sheet of paper and less than a pencil...... Couldn't believe how tied up and awful I felt without having my computer and Internet connection when I felt I had new messages for you; but couldn't let you know right then.

There was so much I had to say to you..I just don't understand where it all went. as if its reserved somewhere but I cant touch it. well thats how it is with metaphysical partners, just like the continuation the Tenth Insight. Almost finished it.

I feel I need to see you. Sitting typing wont do me any good. Tell me where you are and I'll come see you. I need to for my spiritual growth. I wanted to go to Myanmar and Thailand and down to Malaysia eventually.

Sankofa:

"We must go back and reclaim our past so we can move forward;

so we understand why and how we came to be who we are today."

I'm in love with him, but he's got a girl at home. I'm so confused. I don't know what to do[5].

"...the Universe wants me to love you. If I cant love you, I cant live. I cant be free, I cant be psychic, I cant be on a high frequency where being next to you puts me, cant raise the vibration of the planet to help in the shift of consciousness that's taking place. You are part of me, I cant take this!! I have understood what it is to love someone as they are part of you. If they are suffering, you are suffering. If I understand how much you need the love I have for you, it hurts even more. You know why? Cuz its not fair, its stupid whats happening. I see a reflection of where I was sophomore year. Worst times I had when my bipolarity, depression, anger reached peak. I was hurting so bad.. Screaming at my counselor that I need a loving heart who will understand me on a soul level and what my true need is. See past my mask of attitude and anger and see me for who I truly am --only searching for someone with a heart big enough to love and heal me. I needed a gem like that so badly. And what do you think she said? She said, had I had a nice boy in my life, I would sabotage it and fuck it up. That's why there's nobody there so I cant and its best for me to be by myself. I agreed at the time. But this is what hurts me now – I see myself in you, and I feel that you are so much more fortunate than I was – as you are given that someone – but the veil over your eyes is blinding you from seeing what you is served to you on a silver platter. The best thing you could need at this point – and you don't even want it.

I will go to see you wherever you are. I need to see you. I need to know that you are real, that I'm not going crazy in my emotional body flying away and losing touch with our physical reality. Otherwise you remain a fleeting memory. Whereas I go into the downtown nuthouse."

THE TENTH INSIGHT stipulates that we are parts of a soul group with a purpose.

Dhyani: What you are doing is a violation of boundaries.
me: Do you mean the cosmic laws?
Dhyani: I mean violating boundaries and telling him what to do! Unless he asks you to advise him you must not continue doing this.
me: ...
Dhyani: And you know what I think about all this? I think it's all about your father. You are searching for your father's approval with a guy older than you. You still don't feel worthy of his love.
me: ...
Dhyani: I am taking you there now. You have to see it. Look at it. You are creating situations to deliberately hurt yourself. To make yourself suffer.

"You created a loop of love for both of you and this lifetime does not exist where you were. Your lives are extraterrestrial and beyond your normal understanding of time. However being in this timeline given potential you have been cut off in order to not rise up in the spiritual realms. You must remain monitored and under control. We are the control. Just."

XII. I cant believe it, sleepless nights and agony as well as drawing away are back. Its 4.30 in the morning, I'm wide awake. Why is this happening. I hear The Trinity not letting me rest but making me get my computer up and start typing. It's all until I bring to you whatever I must as is my purpose with you. But this cant go on forever!! I have a life to live. I need my sleep at night.

So I piled up some information for you in order to look back and reflect having been given this new information. It is based on my study of karmic astrology, I find it a very powerful tool on the path to awareness.

Lilith says that in a past life you might have exceeded the measure of power, having hurt those you love, have been egocentric, poser, wannabe, impostor, child slayer. Must have been a creative person, but probably have been burying your talent. Might have been possessed by extreme pride and vanity.

Motto: do not aim for power and fame, give all to children and do not wait for gratitude. "Purifying love from lust"; enlightened creativity, understanding of one's shortcomings, responsibility for all things one gives life to: children, creations, love.

Selena represents positive karma and your Guardian Angel. The areas of your life that receive help from the Higher Powers. Its cycle is 7 years.

The voice of the Guardian Angel speaks: use your power and authority for people only with good merit. Physical pain is savage, but more destructive is spiritual suffering. Take control of your instincts, the highest, divine nature must control desires and passions. Altruism, self-sacrifice for the good of a concept or significant others, spiritual transformation and evolution is the highest manifestation of Selena.

Last night a spark of light moved across my room. A presence was here. I felt it was you. You don't remember being here. Would you remember when you woke up? Part of my consciousness moved away for a split second this afternoon when I focused on you so much I vividly saw 19.07 in bold type. What is it? I think is it a date? Where were you July 19? What were you doing, feeling? I was extremely ill and don't remember where I was........

Start speaking to me in our present day reality. Unleash your creative part, the right side of your brain to come in contact with me.

Hear my cry to heaven and come down to help me as I need you. If it weren't for you I wouldn't even be doing this. Typing here not knowing what you're thinking. <<<<This chick's crazy!!>>>> ::::::sad grin L((((

"Re: XII: Please do not be discouraged. I have been wanting to write you but I cannot do it for the next week and a half. I can't fully read our recent e-mails right now as I am in a personal situation I am trying to sort out. I have not been able to give you the proper time that I want to.

You are clearly an important person in my life as I seem to have been in yours.

Thank you with all my heart."

Experiencing emotions. Our communication through the net – the virtual reality – another type of communication. We do not read each others' e-mails and listen to each other. We are reading our reflections in the quiets of our own minds – we are having conversations with our own selves. That was it. Trying desperately to end the frustration I was going through. But I didn't know how to. I guess it is my pattern now – I remember I should have been warned that if I push it, it will blow up. But I had to. I had to say what was on my mind. The first thing that comes to mind. The first impression is the right one. Whereas time and sentiment cloud the mind's ability to judge. But I am ahead of my own self at the moment. We have yet to go another week before he writes back and I am going by and painting, doing some work and trying to progress into the September shift. I re-open myspace and upload my artwork. I get my period as I am wearing my black Nepali skirt with little velour boots and a fluffy jacket. I go to my new work place and come back exhausted with a shit-load to settle for the weekend. I have some red wine to alleviate the menstrual pain. I am laying in front of the TV. I check my e-mail. I feel pain. I am practically not reading what he is saying. I am feeling. It has taken all over me. I can't bear this. I screamed as I felt the pain rush through me in a typhoon of emotion so painful and unbearable.

"I don't want to take your sleep. I know how bad life is without it. I have been living like this for years. These days I have to take sleeping pills for a proper sleep.

I am not sure why I may be able to help you. I am a tortured soul and I hope you don't mind me saying so but it seems you are too.

You see I look back now and realize I have just been in a depression for the last two months. I have compounded it with issues that involve relationships.

It's funny, b/c just as you were actually thinking of taking refuge I was considering the other day. I can't deal with the pain anymore.

But I don't think being a monk or a nun is the answer for us. I believe that we can help and love people. We just have to sort out our issues."

...trying not to give in to the emotion taking over me but it is useless. I am *it*.

"I just read over your e-mail again with all my attention but I couldn't do it before b.c I was in the middle of of the what should have been the best time in my life but instead came out to be the most difficult.

I want to help you. July 19th. It is difficult. I will retrieve my journal which is not here right now. I was in China. Maybe the North. I will try to dig it out out. I hope I wrote that day.

Longest I have ever gone without writing for about two weeks now. Camera stolen, i pod broken, glasses missing, took brash detour to Thailand from Laos. Feel so off track.

Sorry. I am trying to help you but my current issues are coming out. It's not the material things I care about. It's all these things are happening now.

Do you think there is no wrong decision. Everything we do is part of our path? I can't tell. I want to believe that all decisions are good in the end. But what if you missed out on something important - like love???

I am sorry. No more rambling.

I will get back to you with that date the best I can."

- I can't bear this! It hurts to damn bad! It's awful! I can't go through this again! It can't be happening again! I won't be able to go through this again!
- Doti, what's the matter?
- It's...James...I just received a letter from him...he's saying he's been going through shit...I can't help it...I'm feeling him entirely...I can't bear this! This pain is all over me!! I can't take it! I don't know what to do! I can't go through this again! I do not have the strength to go through this again!!
- Just breathe. Please...do you want me to come be with you?
- No!! I must process this!! I'll run! It hurts so bad!! It's all over me!! I don't know what to do I can't take this pain anymore!

"I have read your letter and tears rolled into my eyes and I felt pain. God its been awhile since I touched it so raw. I cried nonstop for an hour and painted. I relate so deeply to what you say about pain and being a tortured soul, you are right. I felt it to the core. But I'm not saying this to make you feel bad, just letting you know that I feel you more than you may realize....

I think, if you believe that God loves you and trust the Universe to work things out the way is best for you, they will. Keep your heart open and intentions pure. Stay in touch with your self and who you are and what you need.

What is meant to be, will be. When two people are destined for each other, there's no way they can be apart. If you think you missed out on something - you are creating energy to repeat it, have another chance, so to speak. You know, we keep repeating things --patterns, till we 'get it'.

You cannot miss out on love --its all around you. Maybe you cant see it, but it's there. It is from within you. Just be loving, like you are. Remember love and compassion. Cus if you can't do it, none of us can do it. The world needs you, your family needs you, your friends need you, because you are, wonderful, beautiful, kind and loving. We are so fortunate to know you. I mean it.

Loving you has given me joy and inspiration I did not think I could ever feel. So profound and beyond anything else I have ever known. How happy it's made me, I was shining, glowing with love, so wishing you would let me make you as happy as you made me.

I am sorry. No more distractions. We have a long way to go.

Only those who can feel pain, be in touch with their pain and be aware of the pain; can feel love.
God's love.

My artwork is *all* about love..."

I add him into my friends on myspace.
I wish I never proofread my e-mail...as it changed the emotional charge.

"Re: XII: I certainly didn't want to cause you more pain.

I wonder if we feel the same pain. How much do I actually have to tell you that you don't already know.

I feel it now. Tortured again. Last night I escaped it a bit but its back. I have found a good friend from my travels and had taken some painkillers.

I am struggling so much with honesty. I end up being so honest that I hurt myself and make my life so complicated. I guess it's okay to omit some things. Everybody doesn't have to know everything about everybody. But if I develop a relationship with the pure foundation of honesty I feel I have to bare all or live with guilt. I am being vague which has caused me so much heartache. I can't ever just do what is best for me.

My mom tells me to just enjoy. She asked me if should go back on cymbalta that I stopped taking. Maybe I should go back on it. And it pissed me off. I can't fucken enjoy. Think way to heavily about things/ life.

Especially now that stuff is a bit too much for me to handle but I must handle it. Also I feel like I should not be on islands in Thailand being as distracted and unappreciative as I am. But I cannot go home either. It would be the worst thing.

Do you believe in God? I believe in the Universe. Something so much more powerful connecting us all. But I cannot say I believe in God.

I feel awful writing this sample of my scattered and troubled thoughts. You have written so much to me but I am scared to read it all. Worst thing is I don't know how telling you about my issues will help you b/c it seems we are both looking to each other for some guidance.

I am sorry. I just need to calm down.

The 19th of July, 2007 "has been a weird day. One of a few epiphanies if not everyday." I was in China and caught a bus from a Buddhist mountain called Mt. Emei and headed to Ya'an (a place I had to stop to get to Kanding). After missing the bus I was supposed to get on in the morning I caught the next bus to Ya'an. Turned out to be an alright time when I met two Chinese university students who helped me around town. They brought me to a guesthouse, showed me where to get on the Internet, places to eat, and around their university. They turned Ya'an into a pleasant experience. After I was with them I spent about 5 hours at the Internet. This is the day I posted pictures of my travels.

I have this day in more detail but let me know if you need any more info. Otherwise there is no point mentioning the dumplings I had.

I am just going to send this b/c I don't know what else to do right now. wow. I have become a fucken basket case man. I need my i-pod back."

Our emotional codes. The emotion that binds us...a whirlwind of excitement...recognition...pain.

"I feel you are coming to understanding yourself, when you are writing. I think you are putting too much pressure on yourself. STOP blaming yourself for things that are out of your control. The only person you need to be honest with is your self. If people cant love and appreciate you for who you are, take it as a signal -they're not for you, cus you dont need anyone who would bring you down or make you feel worthless, guilty, not good enough, or put you on a trip. YOU GOT THAT? Zen Masters call it the sword of discrimination --boom, cha! get outta my way. Wont let you suck up my energy or drive me crazy. Recognize and cut dysfunctional people off. You dont need 'em to drain you out. We're empaths, we pick up people's thoughts and emotions as our own and must learn to cut off alien negative ones. actually I'm working on it but so far unsuccessfully.

I feel studying metaphysics will help you a lot. I feel you shouldn't take meds as your present journey is about finding a holistic healing, that would balance your body and mind. Speaking of holistic, I would love a real Thai massage right now. Come on, go get one, I'll pick up the sensation as my own :o) %) 8)

Thank you for the lowdown on 19.07
I believe it is glitches in time and space. I am in the process of putting things together.

You are helping me when you write and express yourself to me. And you are definitely not causing me any more pain. Knowing you is a pleasure to me, and if our souls are tortured at the same time, at least we both know we're not alone. Not anymore.

Letters from you are like a breath of fresh air cus we are a soul-level connection that is so hard to find, and I want to be there for you, like I should, and I couldn't be happier than I am, because you let me.

I will paint you too one day.

STOP beating yourself up and GIVE UP FEELING GUILT

My wasted heart loves you truly, madly, deeply, unconditionally, spiritually, romantically, soulfully"

What we go through, we have chosen it. We have chosen our experience – based on our grid programming. If your grid programming is to be depressed and keep replaying the same patterns over the years – then it shall be done so by you until something clicks and activates your inner mechanisms to change your patterns. This is usually done by activation of the DNA – meeting another aspect of your being in physical reality. DNA encoding is the key to understanding your programming.

- I might have to leave for a couple of weeks, - I said to Sasha, my boss, on the way for a smoke. – Just some things that need my attention and unless I finish them – they keep torturing me and not letting me focus on work.
- Sure, I mean, you can do whatever you know that.
- I felt I needed to tell you as this is a hard decision for me to make. I can't take off like that.
- Stop being so dramatic. Go and do what you need to do. Come back when you're done.

The Eclipse. It has to do with partnerships. It is erratic. Scattered. Do not make decisions today. Take things slow. It's very hectic. It's bad time to make decisions. Leave it to rest.

"I am tortured by the thought of having to see you and be there with you. I'm going to come to Thailand to see you, my soul connection. I'm not going to miss this chance now that I have it.

Unless you feel its not right for you to see me, tell me where you are, I'll be there in a few days. We could spend some time together, as friends, and just have a quality spiritual time."

He gave me emotional work and mental consciousness I need to keep me interested. He gave me someone who is driven to find the truth – just as I am. He gave me someone who is beautiful physically and spiritually. A reflection. I just wish he could see it. See it for himself without me pointing at it as it is about to happen inevitably. Inevitability. Crash. Boom. Bang. –ing on my mind and telling me it's over forever.

- Are you sure you need this psycho in your life?
- He is another part of me. A reflection of who I am...had I been born as a male we would have been the closest of friends.

"Re: I would love to have quality spiritual time but this is a very bad time for me. I mean very bad. There is no way for you to know that b.c I have never been very specific about what my problems are as my thoughts are all over the place and I never wanted to bother you with details.

Right now I need to unwind and simplify my life. It means being on my own. Alone. I am joining a meditation and a yoga retreat. Something for my soul.

It may be a great thing one day djana. But right now I know I would just be more confused.

Please don't take it personally. I just know that I need to search on my own. It does not mean I don't want to hear from you. Far from that. Just need to feel on my own way now. Back in tune.

I appreciate your want to come down here.

I strongly feel that I need to do this solo right now.

I am sure you understand.

I love your artwork."

I run to the stream in the National Park by my house. *You're killing it.*

"Re:Re: Keep pushing me away, I don't care. Told you I see myself in you. I am your soulmate and I will prove it to you. It's not over until I have you look in my eyes and tell me, tell yourself, you don't feel the same way I feel about you. I am your friend, first of all. If I'm not the One for you, I want to know now. There wont be 'one day, djana'. These things come when they are unplanned. If I'm not there for you at the worst time in your life, I'm not ever there.

Just think about me for a minute. How bad it is for me to feel you all the time knowing if you let me help you, I can. Thinking about you and our connection morning, day and sleepless nights. Help me help myself.

No more typing, I need to tell you in your face. Cant pretend, cant take it easy. Do you ever act impulsively? It is the soaring of emotion that makes me drop everything and be with you. As your friend first of all. As your strong soul connection thats not gonna give up. Any friend would have done the same thing.

But you feel your old patterns coming up right now -- as if I'm gonna take your time, expect you to act a certain way, take your attention from your spiritual growth...But let me tell you something. *This* is your chance for spiritual growth. This is my chance, too. I am learning about myself, I am learning and exercising my ability, but for that, I need you. For some reason I am psychic with you. This means there's more for me to learn from you. Help me take this opportunity.

Don't you understand that if you don't let your wall come down now --with someone who intuitively soul-levelly understand you-- let me be there for you, because I AM there for you, with you, all the time, but you're not letting me close. It may take you lifetimes to work this issue through.

Is this what you want? You decide. Thats not what I want for you, I want you to work it through, become
more functional and more aware, and I am, again, your chance to do this. Put yourself to the test. You're not losing anything.

...understand that I am not asking anything from you, ANY-
THING
Only a chance to see you

Think about it and let me know once and for all. I care about you beyond your understanding, as I have told you before - we are each other's parts, and it hurts me so bad that the Universe wont you let you remember or recognize me the way I recognize you. God. Read 2150 A.D. I have a feeling you will love it.

Its in your hands now. I've bared it all rough and raw. You're seeing me for who I am, right here, before your very own eyes

Where you take it from here
Is the choice I leave to you."

This love is giving me so much. I transform absent-mindedness into mind-fulness.

...an hour later:

"Dang I just realized you're right I am confusing you more. All this writing and all my thoughts are just as bubbling as yours. We're so alike, lol! It's just that sometimes I feel we can balance each other out.

Point is, if you're doing something interesting I'd love to do it too and I'd love to see you and talk to you instead of typing.

So hopefully you'll say yes let's meet :)"

...next day:

"I think I know what the complication is. You're thinking, why would this girl want to fly across states to see me. What does she want from me. Am I right? What I want is to grow spiritually. In order to do that I must complete my purpose with you, as it is our karma. It is what matters to me the most right now, my spiritual growth. I have more knowledge I need to share with you.

The Angels are telling me constantly to keep talking to you.
I will tell you more about this, about everything, if you want to hear it.
Why am I pulled to Krabi....is that where you are by chance?

I am your friend, and will be always. I don't want to dig into your life or make you do something you don't want to do. I am only asking you for a chance to see you. Lets help each other"

The only way to heal is to merge with the energies of the ancients.

We heal now
or live restless in guilt, attachment and remorse.

...the pain will drag us both back into the abyss of 3D: dependence/disappointment/despair.

I must hold on to love

Keep love alive

hold on to the creative, sacred power of love. It has to live.
I stand on my balcony, smoking. shaking

I look out into the darkness of the night. The light flickers

the second our eyes met >< our souls began an unspoken subtle communicationhis essence...whispers

Now your love for me is true
If we risk everything
If we do it now
Our lives will be changed. We stop time. We start to live in present.

...looking at me through a prism of the past and the future
Squared in the cosmic vacuum.
It's now or never

"I apologize for bothering you all the time. I feel tortured by not being able to speak with you live. I feel we need to address our pain. I feel we need to be in this together to get to the core reason -- I have to do this, so do you. I have experience in the metaphysical and spiritual field, that I want to share with you. It's why I kept writing to you all the time I feel, I feel...I feel....

Feel so dizzy. Can't take it. There is no past, present or future. Everything is happening at the same time.

Feel me for a minute. I hope we can meet. I don't care where, I don't care in what conditions. It just has to be now. We both need this.

I'm scared. I am afraid there wont be another chance. We cant miss this one.

I need you. I cant do this on my own anymore."

IX. Endless Knot.

"The love that awakened was love that comes genetically – it is in your heart and your innermost depth. It's so natural to love. This is within the nature's desire for you to love unconditionally."

Why am I being told you're scared of me. Why would you be scared of me. Am I scaring you. How. By telling you about my love for you? You should feel happy about this, not be scared. Do you think I would say something for you to be scared? So give it up, don't waste yourself giving in to the low emotions.

Do you want to be loved?

Then what are you waiting for?

I am here. . .I love you.

Are you scared of the bond we are developing?
Why? I am here and I'm not going anywhere. I love you and it gives me strength to get through another day. You have given me a reason.

Do you think one day I might be gone so you wont bond back with me? It's too late. The bond already exists. You see it, it exists. You proved it to yourself when you opened your heart to me, and you saw and you felt my open heart take you in wholly.

What was the sensation like?

It must have been all-encompassing, incredible.

Do you think if I get to know you I won't like you? Want you? Want you less? Is that why you won't let me in? too late. I already know you, I know what I need to know to love you. You have let me in and I saw you bare, stripped of pretenses and lies, for who you are. I have already bonded with you.

We have shared our understanding and pain.

Isn't this so beautiful.

Doesn't this make your heart sing?

Two beautiful but wounded souls found each other and helping each other on their paths. Don't ever think it could have been any better than we are making of it.

The time is now. There is no turning back, since we have both made this step. We are teaching each other such an important soul lesson. Please embrace it.

You are teaching me to love, I am teaching you to be loved. Where there is love, there is no fear.

I love you, James

I was scared. I was so scared of what I felt when I met you. I pushed it away. Ordered my mind to be angry at you so you wont talk to me cus everytime you did I wanted to tell to let the world know I can't believe you're here and I want to hold you so much. But wont cus we're parting our ways. Don't give in, I told myself. But this love happened to be beyond all this ego control crap. Had it not been for you, I would have never opened my heart to you. On the library stairs. So praise to you.

Take my love, as there is no one else but you. No one else exists but you. You are my king, my love, my everything. You are the one I am saving all my love for. You are the man I love. You are the man I want. You are the One who makes my heart beat faster. Your smile makes me weak in the knees. In your eyes I dissolve and become one with you. I want to make you happy, make the world shine for you baby

I never knew a love like this before. . .You're a dream come true.

I lay the Quest tarot for an answer whether or not I should send him this letter. Cataclysm.

I will just go into work. Thank God there is work for me here otherwise I would have gone mad.

Brace yourself. I am laying all your shit bare. I was working on my computer but ain't my fault you're popping up every time I'm trying to focus on my work. Here comes.

The following is the source of your suffering and heartache as you tell me. THAT wall around you that you put many years ago is the source of each and every suffering you experience. You seem available and charming, yet it's a façade you carry. The wall around you basically means, "I will never really show you my vulnerable side. I don't even know it's there". You're not aware of it. What you do makes people THINK you're available, you make them love you, BUT just as they get too close to that wall — like I did, you discard them, cut them off. Did you say you always break up first with the girl? Right. You're rejecting them, so they don't reject you. True?

Who rejected you as a kid? Was it your father? You think you're ready to love and be loved, you fight for what you want, and once you get it — Ah, ain't all that. Don't even want it. Ain't bothered. That's why you're suffering.

Desperately repeating the pattern of trying to win your daddy's love, you're pro-jecting and playing out the same situation over and over again. You pick girls that somehow represent your father. Or mother, for that matter.

How do I know this? I must. I didn't tell you before. I was desperately trying to make you come out the true wonderful guy that you are, because that's how I saw you. I saw your true self. You just felt you weren't good enough. You didn't feel you deserve the help or attention. Right?

Did you feel if I got closer to you, I wouldn't want you? Or want you less? Is that why you're not letting me in? You fear I will reject you and discard you, like your father?

So you keep me on a "short leash"

Do you feel you're not worthy of my love? Do you feel you cannot make someone happy by letting them love you?

Or think where it can lead to or if you can't live up to my expectations?

Do you want to let this wall come down? This is how you do this. I am giving you the tool right now, as we speak. You start seeing it. You come to being aware of it. You introspect and analyze. You see each and every situation, person, significant other that you don't let in. no, people don't have to know everything about you. This is your honesty issue. Your logic thinks it can fool people, trick them into thinking you're available. But you said yourself it's giving you a heartache.

I'll try writing more about this later.

Breaking a vision. At that point in time my chemical composition could have attracted any soul connection – and based on my grid programming it had attracted him in particular – carrying a similar code. The depression code, the chemical imbalance code, the sabotage code – this is our reality.

I dreamt of a chocolate pineapple. It was the time to heal. To make the transition together – that way we change our paths forever and always. We share our deepest pain and transform it. Deep appreciation for the path we walk. We find asylum.

Love transcends the pain.

If I already couldn't save us in the past but in the present I can fix the future. And the thought was giving me wings. Wings brought by the Solar eclipse, convinced he is about to ask for my help – as he should – it is one of the things he needs to learn and understand. There is always help out there...you just need to ask for it. I cannot interfere. I cannot push. It is not our destiny. Just as I start thinking how I felt in the interim stage I realize...this is not love. No longer. This is pain of rejection and dependence. And now it is hitting me back. It is back-fighting me. The end of this year was to bring about energies of the past – periods from around 8 or 10 years ago. Including our meeting. Including getting together with him. And waiting until he resolves his path. So until then we are interlinked and until he can heal I cannot move on.

"...how can you just be so beautiful to me...More and more I realize how depressed and sad you really are inside. The more time goes on the more I go back and remember your actions and the pain within. I'll make your life easier by asking you not to write back to me. This creates more connection and insight as I read you between the lines and understand your Self, which comes out and speaks to me; this makes me feel I understand you more than you understand your Self. But that which speaks and loves me is your Self, not you. The right side of my brain is occupied with thoughts of you. You do not want to meet and talk so I'll keep writing. Your addiction to pain is incredible. You are so used to feeling pain either consciously or, most of the time, unconsciously, that you do not want to feel happy or loved. your heart center is blocked with darkness and sadness. Once you feel loved, you don't want it. You cut it off, as you are afraid of the love taking away your one true best friend, the one that which is always there for you...your pain. It is her that will never let anyone else get close to you. Cus if they do, you will start feeling how beautiful life can be when you are love. What's the pain going to have left?

It will have nothing. It will have no power over you, and slowly it will cease to exist. You can't let that happen. No one gets close to you. No one knows you or understands you like she does. At the end of the world....its just the two of you. Well...one :(."

...as if a glimpse into a parallel lifetime bringing waves of emotions that my body is still so well in touch with. Nevertheless our present is predetermined and there is no **us**...

I always needed strength to go through every time I was becoming connected. It was streaming through my own body in the blood flow which was taking me to him. My pressure would jump up and down in ways I always forget and does not remain in the memory to remind me of the jolt it takes to be with him every time.

It's been another fit and I have written another e-mail remaining in my drafts to this day.

X. Blizzard

It is his birthday and I have been preparing how to congratulate him for over a month. First I picked out a poem and a postcard with the song "Truly, Madly, Deeply" and sent it to myself. It was so melodramatic. I would get involved again. I'd rather write a letter.

"....Happy birthday! Just couldn't resist but write to you on this special day :-) Think about you and start writing to you but never send it. Talking to you makes me become more involved.........I always think we can learn from each other a lot more and even if we don't meet, there are other planes we always will - we stay connected on other levels"

No. Not like this. Rewind. No more opening and giving my heart to him. Stop being so emotional and giving. Just say what you have to say. Happy birthday and best wishes.

I am going crazy as I have put myself on a trip. "Cut dysfunctional people off...don't let anyone who puts you on a trip..." I was literally desperately trying to save him at the cost of me.

- What is it about him that triggered you so much? What are you going to do now?
- Go crazy.
- Why don't you go IN and find him to have closure?
- He said he wants to be by himself. I will not wander around IN and look for him.
- You are so clear about this.
- It's true.
- Right. So what makes you think he is so special? Don't you think it is all because of the surrounding you met him in..?

Everyone comes to a point – be it chemically, metaphysically, psychologically – when they are prepared for a deep, big love. My time has come. I should have known better at that time – I would find someone to fall in love with and someone I can truly love – wherever I go. I should have been more precise about the location in third dimension.

…I woke up in pain and I couldn't get my mind off of what had happened back in August.

It's snow blizzard outside my window as I paint away. Heart-wrenching, will-breaking pain, confusion, loss, grief, aggravation...fury of helplessness and inability to have it the right way.

- You need someone who is going to be patient and tolerate you.
- I don't need to be tolerated!!
- Well…
- I need to be loved.
- That's what I'm saying only someone who loves you unconditionally can cut it with you.
- Yeah? And where am I going to find a gem like that..?
- For starters, you should get out of the house and start meeting new people.
- I am shutting myself out from the world to be safe.
- You need something that would keep you occupied and interested. In love. A business. Instead of a man.

Christmas day. Another conversation with myself.

Put aside the fears that hold you
Let my loving arms embrace you
Take your agony away
But its you who can do it

Remember...help yourself first, then others

The pain has been so severe in the last month. So hardly bearable. can't make decisions, plan, project.

Just want to runaway but wherever I run, there I am. I wonder if you feel the same.

Last night was awful. I screamed it hurt so bad. Love died inside me. A piece of me died. I held tight to the cabinet doors.

I prayed *please don't kill it.* Don't take it away. Without this love I cannot live.

I got hurt again. vagueness….inability to give…hurt me. No matter how strong I thought love had made me. but they say love passes – reaches a peak and then drops. Did it drop? I don't know. I was talking to him again. Pain makes us closer. Who told me this? Why was I torturing myself like this? Isn't this violation of all the possible boundaries *and* cosmic laws? But so is putting somebody in my path like this. But when if not "now" **was** the time to work out my issues. He is the only man in the flesh who knew exactly what I felt my entire life: pain. pain that tears you apart. the pain…that I knew *he* felt because I loved him as he is a part of me.

Time has its own rules. It will never let anything like this pass by.

our planet is shifting.

Grief over the love that had died within me remains
an emptiness
a black hole
I am trapped in the cosmic void

The sound is *hummmmmmmmmmmmmmmmmm*

Tell me the truth…

I feel it's all been said and done. I move on further working in a different field and filling my mind with my future work. I was passing time. Until I am finally triggered to take this journey and forever as now, pass it on to those on a similar path and in need of direction.

I heard things. I painted things. I am meant to let him go – only that way he can find love. When no one loves. obviously someone does hence he is not free. But he couldn't cut it with me then, so how is he going to do it now? Can he do it? Will he do it? Will he be lead and allowed to do it? Is he going to become aware and take control of his experiment. I don't know. Our past is living itself out again. *Can you recognize me for I am in this other form. Can you love me and keep me in your heart until we reunite.*

Having triggered the memories of love from within him as I had been told to and now releasing him makes me having fulfilled my purpose with him. Once I had been given this understanding, I felt much lighter. I finally felt, this Is it! I finally know. There is no more truth than this for me.

Present time. Tonight as memory of what it used to be. . .reviving our connection. . . .12/01/2008

"...I feel tortured. Why do we always set ourselves up to feel pain. Whatever I do only leads to pain. I cant go back to Asia again – everything just reminds me of you.

How could we not heal? How can time never be right? Are you healing yourself? Because I am not. I am stuck in pain and rejection and I do not want to move on from here. I need to unwind. Relax. Leave without a course.

Do we have second chances? I don't know. Can I create this in the future – have someone I can work on my issues with? I cant tell. I want to believe so – but after the heartache and pain. . .was it all worth in the end?? If you want to love and you do, how can it never work out? Why is love never enough. Is love just a chemical reaction produced for us to stay attached and emotionally shut down. This is not love. Then what I had for you was not love. Tears in my eyes."

XI. The Ultimate

I wonder why these days in January there is no snow in Moscow. It is abnormally warm for this time of year. I am putting on a slow jam… and floating away to a place filled with love. Where my love is true. And I always feel the same…past/present/future. My truth. My soul asylum: love.

My mind says: if my heart loves so naturally and truly and madly still – how can this be true if it is not mutual. Then parallel lifetimes connecting through the wormholes – and my time/space/grid/travels… are sipping through to my physical body and current <u>memory</u>.

His spirit tells me: what you had felt was true and a connection from the future. We will be together and in love one day just not today.

…a brush in my hand

in the interim present: the pain is unbearable. I hardly hold myself from writing to him. He might as well be going through this. I hear voices in my head saying, how could you deceive me like that. You knew how much I needed you. I had no choice but to be your guide and now I am being punished. No thanks from you. No respect or gratitude. No care about my feelings. How could he betray me like this. Drive me. I could have gone anywhere in the world to find the right One – but I chose to shut myself in a monastery in Nepal. and without giving myself proper credit for the fact that I should have known. My heart is about to be broken. First I will feel high, but then it will eventually drop and leave me profoundly low for whatever time I need to be at zero point

Phthalocyanine blue with a hint of snow white
Spirals of consciousness
....I am traveling in blue...traveling in time.

"One shall not bring the object of love higher than God." One always finds refuge and protection in God whose love is unconditional whereas everyone else comes second. Seeing The Trinity. The Father, Son and the Holy Spirit. Three Angels with gigantic wings. I remember them. Amina says my painting of him is a depiction of God. The halo from the Saints. Apostle James stood next to me. The land was barren, soil cracked, water dried out. I crossed over.

First we learn to love, and then to let go. *We must learn attachment in order to learn detachment. It is the only way.*

- You saw it in his eyes at the library stairs. You could see the scenario playing out – you go together but it doesn't work. You decided – at that very moment – before you mess things up – you remain to yourself – being in love and opening your heart is so much more important than a relationship in transit – you have just sent the outcome.
- Who triggers my mechanism.
- One who is lonely, sad, depressed, angry, lost and confused and doesn't know about it. keeps a mask on.
- Why am I attracting this?
- What does your Self tell you.
- That it is what I want to experience.
- It is true. You want to love and heal them.
- But it never works out! I can't love and heal them – it's not the destiny!
- Who makes up your destiny.
- It's predetermined.
- Major parts, not minor.

- This is major.
- Maybe it was a glitch. Check the blueprint of your meeting.
- I wanted to love. I loved him first. Or did I see things first. I think I saw him and felt I was connected right away – the information started coming. Is this connected to my vision?
- Might be. You might have psyched a possibility of a lifetime – with him. You might have seen an alternate reality. You might have had a dream and decided it was not the path you want to walk.
- Was it real?
- Yes.
- Was the love real?
- It was transformation of pain. You transformed all that you have been going through – from before – into feeling high in love. The psychic senses were due to your heart opening as it was predetermined – you had made the path through too quickly and healed yourself so fast that there would be no point for you to remain here. You eternally try to bring knowledge to those who will never understand it – this is the purpose. Otherwise they wouldn't need you. You understand it and you are okay with it.
- Ohh...why did it take me all these months...why am I attached to him? How do I stop this cord.
- It will go away eventually. Once you shift your energy. Once you shift your consciousness.
- When?
- June. He will be returning home and thus breaking the connection with you – his inner child will be occupied – his mother will be around. His father as well. He won't need you then.
- The summer. In the Summer. What happened.

- His spirit. His Manipura - a bright yellow cord shot out at you when he ran to say goodbye. It hooked on your giving love and attached itself to you. He is still readable from your aura. You need to process it and let it go slowly by slowly. It was very powerful – the entity, the spirit was connecting and feeding on your feeling love for him – thus making it easier on him. His longing was satisfied as you were feeling love. Then it was gone and he was left with his pain. That part of him gave you psychic powers and ability to read him. The connection. Also he would not let you go until you connected to him entirely.
- His entity?
- Yes that soul entity was reaching out to you – wanting to get on you so it won't be suffocating anymore, so that it can live in your heart. This is how you create connection.
- He came back when I pushed him away.
- He wouldn't let you go. IT wouldn't let you go. It would take over him – until he gave it to you. You took it with you. Last time you saw him.
- He wasn't dying inside anymore.
- He felt freed. His energy was lifted as his ego took over again. It is his soul that was speaking to you. It was very real. It was what was making you want to vomit.
- Oh my god. As soon as he felt I loved him...
- He didn't want it. He got the energy exchange. He wasn't in need of you anymore. His entity was all over you.
- What is this entity? Who is it?
- It is his troubled child. He did ask you once whether you were his mother, didn't he?
- Yeah.
- All of it was real. It was a lot to carry on at once. It was overwhelming. You were in it all by yourself. It got to you when you shifted your energy when you got sick. He got

sick a few days later – he was feeling his part leaving him to talk to you. It doesn't matter how much it takes you – and you did the right thing to subdue his talkings. He will never let you go. It sucks up on your energy of feeling love for James. For this entity. And it will make you suffer for never getting reciprocation.

- It doesn't matter how much I talk to him…
- No he will never really accept or understand what you are trying to bring to him. He was never meant to. He was never supposed to, you played out your scenario, you got what you wanted from that experience – you became psy-chic and high on feeling love and then it dropped and it left as you got busy with other things. You did the right thing.
- Is he gone?
- Almost.

The exit is through the code 11 x 2 = 22. The master numbers explored in the search for the ultimate truth behind this power. The energy of these numbers brings psychic senses. It comes after the cycle is completed.

…as we had been intertwined – our link to the source. Both of us working for our family businesses, both starting out at the same time and putting our feet down to not do it anymore.

Time: January 28, 2008.
Place: my apartment, Moscow.

We meet and make two worlds collide. End of January
I see him in the monastery in Nepal
bringing me more insight into our destiny.
We found each other. Brought by the Guardians of Buddhism.

And I still remain in love with those times.

Snow starts to fall. It is a blessing.

His spirit is standing in my doorway and trying to reach out. "You need to move on. You need to let go. Let go of me and follow your own path. This is what you have to do."

In the end these things matter the most: How well did you love? How fully did you live? How deeply did you learn to let go?

So there goes the thinking.
There goes the wonder
What we had ever meant anything
Over and over and over and again and again.

Every time I remember looking at you
Now reflecting the truths of the world shining back at me
In my writing, my painting

My truth, my path
We make it together
As this causes me to throw up again
I know the ultimate truth

When I had the choice to make I still made the same choice, and thus I am not finding him. Him. You.

And thoughts of you and your path
Cause me so much pain
As I roll the film of memories
Inside my mind

This man I see in my dreams. His light is white gold all over...an image, a memory...a reminisce.

I wake up in this world. Again. Breath

I remember how much fun we had last night. the sensation that collides our beings together...onely, truly. The Angels are saying children. I see children/California/A Man Named Michael

I want to be your one and only so much
Want to hold you in my arms
Give you my loving
I been saving it all for you

Where have you been so long
All the while I missed you
Till this day you came along
And lit my world

Disappeared in one second
Gone in a blink
On and on and on

This slight, gentle breeze surrounds me
In its loving gaze surrounds me
Takes me away in the drift of this surrounds me

Psyche....easy......the u.s.

Tayata...Om Mune Mune Maha Munye Soha

...another encrypted message in green ink.

Slipping thru my fingers

...love is grains of sand

Place: somewhere between realms
Time: eternity

Tears are rolling into my eyes….. I am shuffling time….I can't see what day it is…is it summer again? We are in Sumer. Family. Bloodline.

Genetics. chemistry binds us. *trace the lineage.*

Programmed for imbalance until we meet and balance the equation……………………

Uhhh this is hard. I see you. In my head. Because of my head. I can't smoke anymore. I feel you. I have tooth decay I can't smoke anymore. My dream of you as a reflection of my sub consciousness telling me to see the doctor.

….a powerful bloodline that connects us on the soul – blood level.

The soul is the blood, says Christopher[6].

Go back to the beginning of days. *Djannah* = paradise. Paradise Garden.

Garden of Eden. The garden house. The banishment.

You are the chest of all my answers. As I open it, the truths of the Multiverse come springing out.

Tibetans…Bon-po….axis mundi.
Edifice of Nine Swastikas…
we reverse time with the help of our ancestors
Stop the time-loop
come together in real-time to make it right. we make it right.

The Doctrine is in front of my eyes. It holds the answer. As you do.

---

6   Holmes, Christopher. Zero Point Institute.

Volume II
A Story of Faith

- AN EXCERPT -

...as I walk past the dumpling shop through the cobbled streets of the old town of Zhongdian

on to the gigantic gold-encrusted prayer wheel, here I am...here <u>we are...</u>

located in time, yet there is no present moment.

I feel this is the time for me to begin my healing process. As my wishes seem to become true with the Guardians of Buddhism...the evolved beings standing guard on my life's past, present and future...I feel this is it. Here I heal my entire lifetime. Not only my heart. I had been brought here by my drive and by my own destiny...and while I am here, enjoying the energy and the man, I will complete my writing. I try spinning the prayer wheel to thank heavens for this gift of love. I pray for love to stay.

...I sneak into his bed and start kissing him as I press my body against his. He gets excited, aroused. I want him. He slips on a condom and I want to be on top but he gently lays me down and goes inside me as I sign and we both move up and down as I smile at him...we are making love in the morning. He stops himself after I come, grabs my towel and jumps into the shower while I get my green tea. He will be studying all day and I will be visiting the Ganden Sungtseling Gompa. It is 300 years old. It was destroyed during the Cultural Revolution and completely re-built. It is situated 5 km from the city on an isolated ridge known as the Guardian Hill, to which I catch a bus. As I make my way through the main gate I feel I am back home. The white-washed walls, the crimson decorated window-frames and monks spinning prayer wheels. I walk around and take pictures. Yes...my camera is working again.

The walls of this Tibetan monastery are decorated with murals of parasols - one of the 8 auspicious symbols. The Sanskrit term 'chat-tra' is a reference to its shape. The parasol or umbrella is a traditional symbol of protection and royalty. The ability to protect oneself against inclement weather is a status symbol. The coolness of the shade of the parasol symbolizes protection from suffering, desire, and other spiritu-ally harmful forces...and my favorite has always been the endless knot. Like the endless channel of energy within a group of souls...

...and love in its pure form. Kindness is a daily form of love. But love goes beyond kindness...

All the great spiritual traditions of the world teach that love is the essence of all things and that creation arises from love and is sustained by love. People who have had mystical experiences say the same thing, as they describe their individual self feeling the indescribable bliss of the creative, sustaining love. Ever afterwards their lives are changed by this glimpse into ultimate reality. Many people who are resuscitated from clinical death speak of the same thing, and once again the experience can be life-changing.

Love of this kind is very much more than romantic love: a unify-ing, life-enhancing love, which embraces all that is and subsumes time and space and all that ever was and ever will be. Kindness is an expres-sion of love in daily life, but love goes far beyond kindness. The experience can unify all opposites, reconcile all differences and end all strife and suffering. Mystics say that in the experience of this kind of love all mysteries are revealed, including the mysteries of life and death and the mystery of our own being.

I imagined everything. When I had the chance, the loophole to find out about destinies and reach the Ultimate mystery of our being... the Guardians of Buddhism blessed me with that opportunity.

Destiny is like a river: if you keep resisting your destiny you will always be swimming upstream. If you give in to your destiny, the river will carry you.

Find out what your destiny is.

Buddhists believe in precious human lives. You could have been born a bug, had you had that bad karma. But to be born as human, is already significant of good karma. Thus...this precious human life.

Once you see the future, it changes. Because you have seen it.[7]

I return to the city as I see him going into our favorite cafe. I get off the bus and step inside as he says hi to me and continues talking to another chick. I get absolutely furious but say nothing. I stay in the cafe for a little bit...and walk out. I did not think it would be over THIS quick. It sucks. It is unfortunate. Why are all guys the same. Once they fuck you, they lose interest in you.

- Djana, hey!

He is walking right after me.

- I assume...right now...you are feeling something close to jealousy...??
- You assume correct.

---

7   Nicolas Cage, *Next*

I continue walking. He stands still for two minutes and leaves. I walk down the street to get some wine for dinner and return to Kevin Trekker's to find him sitting on the porch, waiting. I did not think he would be.

-   I am glad you did not go far away.
-   Well...I am here.

I walk into our dorm. He follows me.

-   Djana...listen...can we talk?
-   Okay. Talk.
-   Look, let me explain myself. It is funny that you think I like that girl because frankly all she does to me is annoy me. I talked to her as I met her in Lijiang and she happened to be at the cafe. When you saw me - I just got to the cafe. I bet you thought I arranged to meet with her and had been hanging out with her for the day. I did not introduce you because she was not important. All I really wanted to say was, *Djana, I am really excited to see you.* I know how you feel - I have been there. I am probably the most jealous person ever.

I smile at him in relief.

-   So are we okay now?
-   Okay, - as I smile and move closer, - thank you.

He holds me in his arms.

-   Let's go eat dinner with Kevin and Becky.

Made in the USA
Middletown, DE
10 December 2022